U0145458

應用外語 02

英文段落
寫作範例

陳怡真
王鶴巘
〔著〕

兩位英文教學經驗豐富的大學教師
精心合著的英文段落寫作教學範本

ENGLISH

五南圖書出版公司 印行

自 序　PREFACE

　　寫作是一門辛苦的課程，不只是學生，任何人想要寫好一篇好的外語文章，除了自己本身的文法底子要扎實、字彙量要夠，還要常常閱讀、涉獵各方面的知識訊息，增長見聞。這樣寫出來的文章作品，才能言之有意，字裡行間亦能讓人知其所言，感受作者的文筆風格。不過要寫一篇好的英文作文，事實上又談何容易？如前面所說，文法與字彙是最基本的外語寫作要件，可是影響最大的卻是每個人的母語，因為我們在構思一篇文章，很難不會先用我們的母語去安排文章內容的起承轉合。不過，既然是學習不同的語言，就應該要努力使用該語言去思考，避免直接翻譯，因為這樣很容易寫出中文式的英文句子。以英文寫作為例，不論是描述、敘述、比較、因果的文體，或是藉由文章表達意見、想法、論述等等，文章段落裡必須要有主題句、支持句和結論句。其實只要掌握這個基本原則，就能寫出一篇英文作文。寫作事實上就是一種創作，有的人一寫起文章，信手拈來、洋洋灑灑、文思泉湧；有的人則絞盡腦汁、腸枯思竭、一個字也擠不出來。在英文寫作上，這兩種情形上多少是因為每個人的字彙、文法、句子的組織能力和生活經驗不同而有所差異。

　　本書的兩位作者陳怡真老師與王鶴巘老師皆在科技大學應用英語系任教多年，陳老師本身又是教授英語寫作課程與擔任碩班研究生論文的指導教授，基於多年的教學經驗，發現學生在英文寫作上遇到的困難包括用字不適當、文法不正確、文章句子缺乏連貫性、不知如何組織全篇文章等等。因此，我們一直希望能編寫一本「英文段落寫作範例」的書，期望能改善學生的英文寫作能力。本書每篇作文是以學生的日常生活事物作為題材，由陳老師撰寫範文，同時每篇範文之後王老師會就重要單字、句子、表達語做文法分析解釋。

PREFACE 自 序

　　總之，我們希望本書不僅是提供準備全民英檢（GEPT）或托福（TOEFL）的學生、科大應用英語系一、二年級的學生，還有教授寫作的老師一本實用的英語寫作教學教材。

　　本書亦附上一張「實用寫作字彙」的光碟。這些是作者們依這些年來的教學經驗，將適合本教材的字彙收集、分類編集成一片光碟，作為輔助學習教材。

陳怡真老師、王鶴獻老師
於南台科大2014

序 言　PREFACE

　　英語早已成為國際共同溝通語言（English as an International Language = EIL），而且非英語母語人士之間或與英語母語人士使用英語做為溝通工具之人數已經遠遠超過英語母語人士之間用英語溝通人數，足見熟稔英語已成為在國際村進行國際交流必備之條件。

　　英語是大家不陌生也歷經多年學校學習之外語，到了大學後還在學英文，但為何大家還是普遍不敢開口說英語，在英文寫作上，更是困難重重？原因其實很簡單。首先，大家平常不必也沒有習慣說英語，說英語變成很陌生不習慣的事情。再來，不必說英語自然就不會有動機練習說英語。現在，大家慢慢感受到英語重要性，進入職場後漸漸發現英文口語表達與寫作能力的重要性，但工作繁忙，很容易找到藉口把改善英語能力擺在一邊。較積極主動的人會利用時間加強英文能力，可是在改善英語口語與寫作能力方面則因為沒有正確方法與實用指引教材輔助，往往依然力不從心，常會半途而廢，甚至不願勇敢面對，甚為可惜。

　　相較於英文閱讀與聽力方面參考書，坊間英文寫作方面實用參考書數量上顯得較少，很多寫作參考書因過於著重文法解析以及忽略學生學習背景，情境與需求之不同而未能真正解決學習者問題，而導致對改善學生寫作能力之幫助很有限。更重要的是，對技職體系學生，很少有寫作教材參考書針對他們的英文程度以及需求來編寫，這對英文能力普遍低落的技職學生而言更增加了語言學習競爭之劣勢。

　　很高興，我的兩位同仁，怡真與鶴巘老師，根據他們過去在英文寫作與指導科技大學應用英語系大學部與研究所學生英文論文寫作豐富經驗，

PREFACE 序言

深切了解到科大學生英文寫作之困境與弱點，進而決定一起編寫這一本對英文寫作教與學兩相宜之參考書，尤其期望能對技職英語教育有實際貢獻。對兩位作者這種造福學子，奉獻教育之用心與理念本人深感敬佩，並覺得與有榮焉。

  本書依據寫作功能為導向，藉由實際範例，引導學生如何從段落寫作開始，逐步正確有效關鍵語句或句型來發展語意，進而達到溝通之目的。本書內容結構充分顧及到一般學生在英文寫作上之困難與需求。此外，怡真老師專長在英語教學與課程設計，而鶴巇則專長在語言學，兩人專長互補剛好能將本書目標發揮到淋漓盡致，相信對英文寫作學習者一定會有釜底抽薪之成效與受益良多之感。

黃大夫 敬序
南台科大語言中心主任
8/23/2013

推薦序 PREFACE

　　能用正確的英文句子和結構良好的段落來傳達訊息或意見，是很多年輕學子英文學習歷程中一個重要但又難以達成的目標；在英文系的課程中，段落寫作則是最基本的寫作功夫。基本工夫沒練好，後面的進階寫作課程就會發生問題。英文寫不好，除了可能是字彙及語法的基礎不好以外，缺乏明確的指引及充分的寫作練習也是很重要的原因。

　　記得讀大學英文系的時候，有一位非常認真教大三英文作文的外籍老師，叫Mark。上他的課蠻辛苦的，因為他每個星期二和星期五的作文課除了討論和練習以外，都會分派作業。不過Mark也很辛苦，每次都會把上次收的作業改完發給學生修訂。當時他教的主要就是段落寫作，也因為有他認真的教學，讓班上同學收穫不少。回想起來，還真是要感謝這位Mark老師。

　　Mark老師用的課本是進口的原文書（可能是美國高中學生的作文用書），書中的範例和解釋都很深，讀起來有點難度。現在有關英文段落寫作的教科書比起那時多太多了，英文版、中文版都有，學生可以有很多選擇。在這書海茫茫中，我想向大家推薦我的二位同事用心撰寫的英文段落寫作的教科書。

　　南台應用英語系的陳怡真老師和王鶴巘老師在外語教學方面已經有很多年的經驗，陳老師對於科技大學應用英語系的學生英文寫作方面的困難與問題更是熟悉。為了幫助應用英語系學生學習段落寫作，二位老師特別編寫《英文段落寫作範例》（Models of Paragraph Writing）一書，書中針對描述、敘述、論述意見、分類、過程說明、比較、及因果關係的各種

不同類型的文章，編寫範文，分析範文結構，提示字彙與片語，並解釋文法及句型，讓學生一目了然。難能可貴的是各篇範文都經過精心撰寫，每篇都淺顯易懂、層次分明；而且文後的文法解析完整、清晰，是一本非常適合初學英文作文者使用的參考。不管你是要參加英語能力測驗或是上課有需要，只要你用心研讀書中的範例，並勤快的練習寫作，你的英文作文能力一定能快速的提升的。

　　好書不在多，能用心研讀才重要。希望這本書能幫你打好堅實的英文寫作基礎。

沈添鉋

沈添鉦
南台科大應用英語系主任
8/26/2013

如何寫作文　Writing

1. 寫作

　　英文將「寫作」一詞稱為 **writing**、**composition**，除了單純的指拿筆寫字，還有組織整理之意涵，也就是下筆之前內心應先有一個想法或是主題，接著取材、搜集資料、反覆思量、字句斟酌，然後編寫成一篇作者言之有意，讀者讀之有感的文章。

　　寫作是每個人都有的經驗，特別是現在五六年級的人都還記得在中小學時代每個星期還有兩節作文課，寫作前而且還得先磨墨，再拿毛筆寫字，學學古人氣定神閒、條理構思，方才下筆行文的氣宇。如果我們拿學習中文和英文的過程相比，先不管前者是母語、後者是第二語言的客觀條件，事實上我們從小學中文並沒有所謂的文法課，小學的國語課程都是被要求做正音正字的訓練，從而做照樣造句的練習，背誦朗讀文章，再憑每個人的慧根，自己體會作者想要表達的意念與情境。尤其到了中學階段，文言文的課程更是強調反覆朗讀，雖有文字解說釋義，幫助體會字句裡的箇中意味，但往往日常生活中的白話文都已經詞不達意，寫不好了，更遑論去了解古人文言文艱澀、深奧、一字多義的簡鍊文體。而有些國文老師為求學生考試作文高分，更會教導學生寫文章要引經據典，形成文白合體看似有程度，實際上雜亂無章，有時不知所云的內容。我們評定一篇文章的好壞，多少是從作者的文筆風格，用字遣詞去做評論，所謂的文法只是看他寫的東西是否讀得通順流暢，有無錯別字，要一般人解釋他的文法哪裡錯了倒是很困難的事，通常人們只會依自己母語的語感說這句話應該這樣講才對。例如，我們可能會聽到小孩子說「*我們一家都是人」，就會跟他講你應該說「我們都是一家人」才對。那其中的句法

原因呢？很少人會去探究。

　　英文的學習就不一樣了，我們一開始就要求要學英文文法，自始有了文法學習的認知，這確實是一件好事，至少我們可以寫出合理的語句，儘管常聽到外國人會說我們講的英文都很學院派、文謅謅的句子，不過我們覺得這倒無妨，畢竟最重要的是讓人先看得懂你寫的東西。至於用字用語是否適當，就需要靠大量閱讀來增加字彙，甚至有機會、在經濟能力許可下，到說英語的國家居住一段時間，耳濡目染，才能學到活生生的語言，書本、字典裡沒有提到的，諸如俚語、新的詞語、外來字等等。

2. 如何寫英文作文

　　綜合上述所言，我們認為要想寫出一篇好的文章，基本的語彙、語法能力是必要的，再來才能談如何寫作。不論是用哪一個語言寫作，首先都是先確定「主題」，也就是作者在文章裡要告訴讀者的事情。再來是取材，搜集資料的工作。例如，描述一個人或敘述一件事情發生的經過，可以是從日常生活中尋找，也可以藉由報章雜誌閱讀、電視新聞報導得知。接下來是最重要的工作：構思。有了主題和寫作題材，再來要仔細想想如何將文章呈現在讀者的眼前。因為是用文字表達，寫作者等於是一位無聲的演講者，演講的風格—其實就是寫作的文體—依需要而定，可以是論說、敘述或描寫等等，但終究目的都是要吸引聽講者或讀者的注意，因此構思的工作就是要將掌握的材料，配合闡述的主題，細心地安排，把講述的內容分成段落，使之層次分明，有條理不紊地表達出來。

　　此外，英文段落寫作我們提出以下幾點建議：

　　(1) 每個段落要有一個主題句點出該段的主題。

(2) 主題句需要一些支持句來對主題句加以說明、解釋、舉例。所有句子都與主題相關。此為段落的一致性（unity）。

(3) 段落裡的每個句子意思要合理、合邏輯的銜接。此為段落的連貫性（coherence）。

(4) 結論句為整個段落的總結，它與主題句相呼應，可以是摘要、意見、或建議。

(5) 寫作時避免重複使用同一個詞，讓文章讀起來單調乏味，但也不要刻意使用生僻的詞，令人難以理解。

(6) 句子的長短應根據所需表達的意思而定，盡可能讓讀者唸起來文句流暢。因此過分地使用帶句號的短句，讓人唸起來很急促，或者是使用太多的關係子句造成句意複雜、難以理解，都應避免。

(7) 正確的使用標點符號。標點的誤用或使用不當可能會引起誤解。有關這一點我們會在附錄詳加說明。

(8) 適當使用連接詞和轉折語讓整個段落有連貫性：

順序	first, first of all, second, next, then, finally, before, after, meanwhile
累積	in addition, moreover, turthermore, on one hand, on the other hand
關於	with regard to, with respect to, regarding, as for
舉例	for example, for instance, such as
反義	however, nevertheless, in contrast, on the contrary
原因	because, since, because of, due to
結果	thus, hence, therefore, consequently, as a result
總而言之	in conclusion, in short, in a word, in brief, to surn up, in summary

目 錄 CONTENTS

CONTENTS 目　錄

目 錄 CONTENTS

描述性的段落
DESCRIPTIVE PARAGRAPHS

　　我們寫描述性的文章，不論所要描寫的是人、物或景色，使用的文字首先最要緊的是能準確如實地表達出他們的本質和外貌。描寫性的文體要盡可能做到下面幾個目標：

1. 生動、清楚明白、簡潔有力。寫作的段落不宜拖泥帶水和使用複雜冗長的句子。
2. 從描寫的第一句就要能吸引讀者，引起興趣，願意繼續讀下去。因此要避免重複單調的句式，或太過於用口語解釋的文筆。
3. 善用形容詞可讓描述的人物或景物更加生動。

　　以下我們列舉出五篇描述外表、內在感覺以及感官的段落文章。人有視覺（sense of sight）、聽覺（sense of hearing）、嗅覺（sense of smelling）、味覺（sense of taste）、觸覺（sense of touching）五官，一篇好的描述性文章自然能夠讓讀者的五官有所感覺，產生共鳴，就好像吃到一顆酸檸檬，口水滋滋流，眼睛眉毛揪一起，酸溜溜地牙齒都快要掉下來了。

　　第一篇及第二篇文章描述的是人（people），第三篇文章描述的是動物（animal），第四篇文章描述的是食物（food），第五篇文章描述的是地方（place）。

第一篇文章 My personality 描述個性特質

第二篇文章 An ideal teacher 描述理想老師的特質

第三篇文章 My pet 描述寵物

第四篇文章 Potluck 描述聚餐及食物

第五篇文章 A favorite place from my childhood 描述童年最喜歡去的地方

1. My Personality

My personality is combined by several characteristics: easygoing, friendly, thoughtful, optimistic, and indecisive. I am an easygoing girl, who[1] always wears smile on my face. When I meet new friends, I might be shy to talk to them at the beginning. However, as time goes by, I would[2] make friends with those who[3] share similar interests or points of views with me. My friends are impressed by my friendly manner and thoughtfulness because I pay attention to what they need or how they feel[4]. Moreover, I am optimistic and always look on the bright side of life. For example, I did not do well on the college entrance exam and enter my ideal university. But I was not discouraged because I believe that God never shuts one door but he opens another. I will cherish my learning experiences at this school. Finally, being[5] indecisive is my weakness. Sometimes I find it difficult for me to make decisions. In a word, I am an easygoing, considerate, and optimistic girl. No matter how[6] I would be changed physically, these individual characteristics would be accompanied with me.

我的個性

我的個性包含這些特質：易與人相處、友善、體貼、樂觀、以及優柔寡斷。我是個總是面帶微笑、喜歡與人相處的女孩。當我遇見新朋友時，剛開始我可能會害羞與他們交談。不過，隨著時間經過，我會與跟我有相同興趣或和我談得來的人做朋友。我的友善和貼心總會讓我的朋友印象深刻，因為

我會去關心他們需要什麼或者他們的感受。此外,我的個性樂觀,總是看事情的光明面。例如,我的大學入學考試沒有考好,所以沒有進入我理想中的大學。但是我並不因此而沮喪,因為我相信上帝每關上一扇門,他會打開另一扇門,我將會珍惜在這所學校的學習經驗。最後,優柔寡斷是我的弱點。有時我不容易做決定。總之,我是一個易與人相處、體貼、樂觀的女孩。不管我的外表會怎麼改變,這些個人特質將跟隨著我。

段落結構 ▶

1. 主題句(topic sentence):第一句'My personality is combined by several characteristics: easygoing, friendly, thoughtful, optimistic, and indecisive.'是主題句,點出作者個性。

2. 支持句(supporting sentences):介於主題句和結論句中間的句子都是支持句,分別說明主題句提到的個性特質。

3. 結論句(concluding sentence):最後一句'No matter how I would be changed physically, these individual characteristics would be accompanied with me.'是結論句。

形容個性的字彙 ▶

英　文	詞　性	中　文
optimistic	*adj.*	樂觀的
pessimistic	*adj.*	悲觀的
easygoing	*adj.*	隨和的
outgoing	*adj.*	外向的
friendly	*adj.*	友好的、親切的

英　文	詞　性	中　文
thoughtful = considerate	*adj.*	體貼的、考慮周到的
considerate = thoughtful	*adj.*	體貼的、考慮周到的
humorous	*adj.*	幽默的
confident	*adj.*	有信心的
dependent	*adj.*	依賴的
independent	*adj.*	獨立的
ambitious	*adj.*	有野心的
generous	*adj.*	慷慨的
creative	*adj.*	有創造力的
curious	*adj.*	好奇的
shy	*adj.*	害羞的、靦腆的
quiet	*adj.*	安靜的
sensitive	*adj.*	敏感的
forgetful	*adj.*	健忘的
decisive	*adj.*	堅決果斷的
indecisive	*adj.*	優柔寡斷的
stubborn	*adj.*	倔強的、頑固的
introvert	*n.*	內向的人
	adj.	內向的
extrovert	*n.*	外向的人
	adj.	外向的

---

1 描寫形容個性的字大部分為形容詞，但這兩個字當名詞時指的是人：introvert, extrovert。

字彙與片語 ▶

英 文	詞 性	中 文
characteristics	*n.*	特徵
discouraged	*adj.*	灰心的、氣餒的
weakness	*n.*	弱點
make friends with	*v. phr.*	交朋友
points of views	*n. phr.*	觀點
be impressed by	*v. phr.*	對～印象深刻
pay attention to	*v. phr.*	關心、注意
the bright side of life	*n. phr.*	生命中的光明面
be accompanied with	*v. phr.*	陪伴、伴隨
in a word	*prep. phr.*	簡單地說
- as time goes by, ~		隨著時間過去

- God never shuts one door but he opens another.

上帝每關上一扇門，他會打開另一扇門。

文法解釋 ▶

❶ I am an easygoing girl, *who* always wears smile on my face.

       先行詞   表非限定之關係形容詞子句

　　在本句中，who是關係代名詞引導形容詞子句，修飾先行詞girl。關係代名詞who前面有逗號，表示非限定，用以補充說明先行詞「easygoing girl 容易相處的女孩」。關係形容詞子句who always wears smile on my face在全句中若去掉，只是少了語意上的補充說明，句法上仍是正確完整的。試比較文法解釋3的句型。

❷ However, as time goes by, I *would* make friends with those who ...

　　助動詞would在本句中表達主詞I之意志，不同於條件句中would表示與現在事實相反，而是表示「委婉」的語氣。

❸ I would make friends with those who share similar points of views with me.
　　　　　　　　先行詞　　　　表限定之關係形容詞子句

　　在本句中，與文法解釋1裡的句子不同的是：關係代名詞who前面沒有逗號，表示限定，those是指示代名詞替代friends，後面由who引導的關係形容詞子句，修飾先行詞those，用來限定什麼樣的朋友我會想交往。要注意的是本句中關係形容詞子句who share similar points of views with me在全句中若去掉，語意上、句法上都不完整，是錯誤的句子。

❹ I would pay attention to what they need or how they feel.
　　　　　　　　　　　　名詞子句作受詞

　　在本句中，疑問代名詞what與疑問副詞how引導的名詞子句作為動詞片語pay attention to的受詞。What在其所引導的子句裡具有代名詞的功用，作為動詞need的受詞。疑問副詞how則沒有代名詞的功用。

❺ Finally, *being* indecisive is my weakness.
　　　動名詞+補語作主詞

　　在本句中，動名詞being後面接形容詞補語indecisive作整個句子的主詞。

❻ No matter how I would be changed physically, …

No matter + how/who/what/where/when + S + V…

意思為「無論…」

No matter who = Whoever   無論誰…

- No matter who he is, you should not open the door.

不管他是誰，你不該開門。

No matter what = Whatever   無論什麼…

- No matter what you say, I will not change my mind.

無論你說什麼，我都不會改變心意。

No matter where = Wherever   無論哪裡…

- No matter where you go, you should let your parents know.

不論你去哪裡，你應該讓你的父母知道。

No matter when = Whenever   無論什麼時候…

- No matter when you come, please give me a phone call。

不論你什麼時候來，請打電話給我。

2. An Ideal Teacher

    My junior high school English teacher was an ideal teacher because she had the following qualities: being devoted to teaching, attending to the needs of students, teaching students with love and patience, and inspiring students to develop their potential. With[1] a responsible and dedicated teaching attitude, she tried to make[2] the textbook content comprehensible to students and provided supplementary materials for us to practice the language. For example, she enhanced our reading ability by[3] highlighting important sentences from English newspapers and asking us to write down the sentences

in the notebooks. **In addition**, she created an enjoyable learning environment by asking interesting questions and designing fun activities in class. **Moreover**, she cared about students' feelings by setting up a feedback session at the end of each class. Students had an opportunity to express how[4] they felt about the lesson. **Furthermore**, she was patient in answering students' questions. Whenever[5] a student had questions, she was glad to help the student and give as much time as the student needed. **Above all**, she never looked down on low proficiency students but[6] developed every student's potential. In brief, she was a devoted, loving, patient, and inspiring teacher[7] who deserved respect and admiration.

理想的老師

　　一位理想的教師應該獻身於教學、照顧學生的需求、有愛心和耐心、並能激發他們的潛能。我的國中英語老師是我心目中理想的老師。她有著負責和奉獻的教學態度，努力讓學生理解教科書的內容，並提供我們語言練習的補充教材。例如，她會挑一些在英語報紙上重要的句子並且要我們在筆記本寫下這些句子來加強我們的閱讀能力。此外，她透過有趣的問題及設計有趣的活動來提供一個愉快的學習環境。還有，她也關心學生的感覺，會在每堂課結束前讓學生有機會表達他們對這堂課的看法。另外，她有耐心的回答學生的問題。每當學生有問題時，她很樂意幫助學生，學生需要多少時間儘可能給他。最重要的是，她從來不會看不起程度低的學生，而是發展每個學生的潛能。總之，她是位有奉獻精神的、有愛心、耐心、激勵學生、應當受敬佩的老師。

段落結構 ▶

1.主題句（topic sentence）：第一句'My junior high school English taecher was an ideal teacher because she had the following qualities: being devoted to teaching, attending to the needs of students, teaching students with love and patience, and inspiring students to develop their potential.'是主題句，點出作者的國中英文老師有這四個特質。

2.支持句（supporting sentences）：介於主題句和結論句中間的句子都是支持句，分別說明主題句提到的特質。

3.結論句（concluding sentence）：最後一句'In brief, she was a devoted, loving, patient, and inspiring teacher who deserved respect and admiration.'是結論句，重述主題句所提到的特質。

4.說明不同特質的每個支持句分別用moreover, furthermore, in addition, above all連接起來。

字彙與片語 ▶

英　　文	詞　　性	中　　文
ideal	*adj.*	理想的、完美的
be devoted to	*v. phr.*	奉獻於、致力於
attend to	*v. phr.*	注意、致力於
patience	*n.*	耐心、耐性
inspire	*v.*	鼓勵、激勵
potential	*n.*	潛力、潛能
dedicated	*adj.*	獻身的
comprehensible	*adj.*	可理解的

英　文	詞　性	中　文
supplementary	*adj.*	補充的
materials	*n.*	教材
enhance	*n.*	提高、增加
highlight	*v.*	標明、強調
notebook	*n.*	筆記本
create	*v.*	創作、設計
enjoyable	*adj.*	快樂的、有趣的
design	*v.*	設計
care about	*v. phr.*	關心、在乎
set up	*v. phr.*	建立
feedback session	*n. phr.*	回饋時段
express	*v.*	表達
above all	*adv. phr.*	最重要的
look down on	*v. phr.*	輕視
low proficiency	*n. phr.*	程度低
in brief	*adv. phr.*	簡言之
deserve	*adj.*	應受賞（罰）
respect	*n.*	尊重、尊敬
admiration	*n.*	欽佩

文法解釋 ▶

❶ *With* a responsible and dedicated teaching attitude, she tried to make the textbook content comprehensible to students.

　　由於介系詞出現在名詞或名詞片語的前面，又稱作「前置詞」。本句中介系詞with表示「具有」的意思。

　　本句是用介系詞片語來組合句子，原本兩個句子：

She had a responsible and dedicated teaching attitude.

She tried to make the textbook content comprehensible to students.

合併而成。

❷ She tried to *make* the textbook content comprehensible to students.

　　　　　　　動詞　　　　直接受詞　　　　　　受詞補語　　　　間接受詞

　　原句帶有被動的意味，也就是說教科書的內容（the textbook content）被學生理解。我們亦可用主動的意思表達原句：She tried to make students understand the textbook content.

❸ She enhanced our reading ability *by* highlighting important sentences.

　　本句中介系詞by表示「方式」、「方法」的意思，相當於 by means of（藉由～；靠著～）。

❹ Students had an opportunity to express *how* they felt about the lesson.

　　　　　　　　　　　　　　　動詞　　　　主詞　動詞

　　　　　　　　　　　　　　　　　　名詞子句（作直接受詞）

　　句子中 how they felt about the lesson 為名詞子句，做動詞 express 的受詞。該名詞子句又稱為間接問句，句子結構要用直述句，也就是說：主詞＋動詞。

❺ *Whenever* a student had questions, ～ …

　　'whenever' 是複合關係副詞。意義上相當於 'at any time when'（在任何時候～）或 'every time when'（每每～）。

❻ She *never* looked down on low proficiency students *but* developed every student's potential.

'but' 是用來表達前後句意義相反或相互對比的連接詞。本範例中，'but' 前面有 never 否定詞；但也有可能前句是肯定，而 but 引導的後句是否定的。說話者心理上比較強調 but 所引導的子句部份。例如：

- He could easily finish this job, but he did not.

他原本可以輕鬆地完成這工作，但是他沒有。

❼ She was a *devoted, loving, patient, and inspiring* teacher.

如果是 coordinate adjectives（並列形容詞）修飾同一名詞，只需用逗號連接起來。如果是 cumulative adjectives（多重形容詞）修飾同一名詞，通常排列順序如下：

- articles（定冠詞）：如 a, an, the, this, that, these, those
- quantity（數量）：如 two, some, many
- opinion（主觀而不同的）：如 handsome, beautiful, lovely
- appearance（外觀／大小／形狀／狀態）：如 big, tall, round, hungry
- age（新舊）：如 new, old, young
- color（顏色）：如 red, yellow, black
- nationality（國籍）：如 Spanish, Asian, American, British
- materials（材質）：如 gold, plastic, metal, wood
- noun（名詞作形容詞）：如 stone (stone church), sand (sand beach)

Ex: These two handsome tall young Spanish boys are my students.

這兩位英俊高大年輕的西班牙男孩是我的學生。

3. My Pet

My pet is a Havana cat, a lovely cat with white and silver hair, large eyes, and folded ears. He is one of the popular short-haired[1] cat breed. I remember that when I first saw him, I was attracted by his appearance. I bought a pretty cradle which was weaved by bamboo. I decorated it with a woolen towel inside and a beautiful lace hood outside the cradle. I prepare good quality cat food, some water, and a plate of sand behind the cradle. I devote[2] all my attention to taking care of him. I must admit that he is spoiled by me. I never punish him when he does something wrong[3]. He becomes more and more disobedient and arrogant. He is crazy about destroying everything and making trouble. For instance, he likes to play hide and seek with himself[4] and mostly loves to hide in my closet or tissue box. He rolls on my clothes or tissue paper to make a mess or even tie a knot on my underwear. The most terrible act that I cannot tolerate about him is urinating on my bed. What is worse[5], if[6] I scold him, he shows an innocent facial expression to me. He is really a smart cat. Although[7] he is a naughty cat, I still love him deeply.

我的寵物

我的寵物是一隻可愛的哈瓦那貓，有著白銀色的毛，一雙大眼睛和向前屈摺的耳朵。牠是受歡迎的短毛貓種之一。我記得當我第一次見到牠時，就被牠的外表所吸引。我買了一個漂亮的竹子編織成的搖籃，用羊毛製的毛巾裝飾它的內部及美麗的花邊罩著搖籃。我準備一些品質好的貓食物、水和一盤貓砂擺在搖籃後方。我盡全力地照顧牠。我必須承認我寵壞牠了。牠做錯事時我從來沒有懲罰牠。牠變得越來越不聽話和自大傲慢。牠瘋狂地破壞和製造麻煩。例如，牠喜歡與自己玩捉迷藏，大多喜歡躲在我的衣櫥或紙巾盒。牠在我的衣服或紙巾上打滾，弄得一團糟，甚至在我的內衣打結。我最不能忍受的可怕行爲是在我的床上撒尿。更糟糕的是，如果我罵牠，牠會表現出無辜的表情。牠真是一隻聰明的貓。雖然牠是隻頑皮的貓，我還是很喜愛牠。

* Special thanks go to Erica Kuo for sharing her experience of keeping a pet.

段落結構 ▶

1.主題句（topic sentence）：第一句'My pet is a Havana cat, a lovely cat with white and silver hair, large eyes, and folded ears.'是主題句，指出作者的寵物是隻哈瓦那貓。

2.支持句（supporting sentences）：介於主題句和結論句中間的句子都是支持句，描述寵物貓的習性以及與牠相處的情形。

3.結論句（concluding sentence）：最後一句'Although he is a naughty cat, I still love him deeply.'是結論句，總結雖然是隻頑皮的貓，還是很喜愛牠。

字彙與片語 ▶

英 文	詞 性	中 文
short-haired	*n.*	短髮的
breed	*n.*	品種
attract	*v.*	吸引
appearance	*n.*	外表、外貌
cradle	*n.*	搖籃
weave	*v.*	編織
bamboo	*n.*	竹子
decorate ~ with ~	*v. phr.*	裝飾
woolen	*adj.*	毛織品的、羊毛的
lace	*n.*	花邊、飾帶
hood	*n.*	罩子
admit	*v.*	承認
spoiled	*adj.*	被寵壞的
disobedient	*adj.*	不聽話的、不服從的
arrogant	*adj.*	傲慢的、驕傲的
destroy	*v.*	毀壞
hide and seek	*n.*	捉迷藏
closet	*n.*	衣櫃、壁櫥
tissue box	*n.*	紙巾盒
tissue paper	*n.*	紙巾、衛生紙
make a mess	*v. phr.*	把～弄糟
tie a knot	*v. phr.*	打結
underwear	*n.*	內衣

英 文	詞 性	中 文
terrible	*adj.*	可怕的
act	*n.*	行爲
tolerate	*v.*	忍受
urinate	*v.*	小便、尿
scold	*v.*	責罵
innocent	*adj.*	無辜的
facial expression	*n.phr.*	臉部表情
nauthty	*n.*	頑皮的、淘氣的

文法解釋 ▶

❶ He is one of the most popular *short-haired* cat breed.

　　本句裡'short-*haired*'是由「形容詞＋擬似分詞」所形成的複合形容詞。這裡的「擬似分詞」是由名詞字尾加上-ed，句法功用上當形容詞，表示「具有～」的意思。例如：

　　- a kind-*hearted* man = a man with a kind heart　好心腸的人
　　- a three-*legged* table = a table with three legs　三條腿的桌子

　　另外本範文：'a beautiful *lace hood* outside the cradle' 句子裡 'lace hood' 是由「名詞＋名詞」所形成的複合名詞。其它「名詞＋名詞」的例子如：

　　- language(Noun) teacher(Noun)　語言教師
　　- evening(Noun) paper(Noun)　　晚報
　　- post(Noun) office(Noun)　　郵局

❷ I *devote* all my attention *to* taking care of him.

'devote'是反身動詞，後面接反身代名詞或名詞詞組，之後再接介系詞 to。要注意的是介系詞 to 後面的動詞要用現在分詞 V-ing。其它相同的反身動詞：

- abandon oneself to　沉迷於
- absorb oneself in　專心於
- dedicate oneself to　致力於
- accustom oneself to　習慣於

❸ I never punish him when he does something *wrong*.

形容詞'wrong'在本句裡是限定的用法，通常是放在名詞前面，但是碰到以下的字：something、anything、everything、nothing、everyone、anybody，形容詞皆放在後面。

❹ He likes to play hide and seek with *himself*.

'himself'是反身代名詞。本句中之主詞與受詞同指一人或同一物時，就用反身代名詞。以下我們列出各個反身代名詞與其對應主詞：

主詞	動詞	反身代名詞
I	*praised*	myself.
You	*help*	yourself.
She	*loves*	herself.
He	*spoke to*	himself.
It (= the cat)	*played with*	itself.
We	*know*	ourselves.
You	*help*	yourselves.
They	*enjoyed*	themselves.

❺ *What is worse, ~...*

what is + 比較級 / 最高級,~...（而且、尤其甚者）

what is more、what is worse是一種固定的表達語、慣用語，語法上具有對等連接詞的功用。例如：

- He is a good teacher, *and what is more*, he earns the excellent teaching award.

他是一位好老師，更甚者，他榮獲優良教師獎。

❻ *If* I scold him, he shows an innocent facial expression to me.

'if'（如果、假如）是表示條件的從屬連接詞。本句中所敘述的是事實，條件句的動詞語態用陳述式（直說法），而不是假設語態的動詞。

❼ *Although* he is a naughty cat, I still love him deeply.

'although'（雖然）是表示讓步的從屬連接詞，同義的連接詞還有：though、even though。

4. Potluck

A potluck is an informal meal that each friend brings a different dish shared[❶] among a group of people. During the years of studying abroad, some friends and I, all international students, would have a potluck lunch or dinner on the weekend. Most of my friends were from Asian countries such as Taiwan, Korea, and Thailand, and a few from Western countries like France, so that[❷] we could taste foods from different areas of the world. One of my good friends, who came from Korea, was good at making sticky rice cakes. I liked the salty flavor and elastic, chewy texture of this dish. In addition,

my roommate was a wonderful cook, and she loved to make curry chicken. I still remember the smell of curry which[3] filled our tiny apartment with aroma, and it really tasted[4] delicious. Moreover, a Thai friend usually brought fried noodles. This delicious dish was a mixture of sour, sweet, and salty flavor. Finally, my favorite dish was Quiche, which was introduced by a classmate from France. Her healthy quiche recipe included low-fat ingredients and fiber-rich vegetables such as[5] spinach, broccoli, and mushrooms. It was really tasty. Therefore, in a potluck meal, friends can not only[6] get together but also enjoy great foods.

聚餐

'Potluck'指的是一個非正式的聚餐，每位朋友帶一道菜與大家分享。在國外念書時，我和一些朋友，都是國際學生，會在週末舉行Potluck。我的朋友多數來自亞洲國家，例如台灣、韓國和泰國，以及少數來自西方國家如法國，所以我們能品嘗來自世界各個不同地區的食物。我的一位好友來自韓國，她擅長做年糕。我喜歡這道菜鹹鹹的味道和有彈性、有嚼勁的感覺。另外，我的室友是一位很棒的廚師，她喜歡做咖哩雞。我還記得咖哩的香氣充滿我們的小公寓，它嘗起來真的很美味。還有，一位泰國朋友通常帶來泰式炒麵。這道美味的菜結合酸、甜、鹹的味道。最後，我最喜愛的菜是Quiche，一位來自法國的同學介紹的菜。她的健康quiche食譜包含低脂肪的材料和纖維豐富的蔬菜，如菠菜、青花椰菜和蘑菇。吃起來真是美味。因此，Potluck不僅讓朋友聚在一起，而且可以吃好吃的菜。

段落結構 ▶

1.第一句先定義potluck這字的意思。

2.主題句（topic sentence）：第二句'During the years of studying abroad, some friends and I, all international students, would have a potluck lunch or dinner on the weekend.'是主題句，指出作者和一些朋友一起聚餐。

3.支持句（supporting sentences）：介於主題句和結論句中間的句子都是支持句，分別說明每道菜餚看起來、聞起來、吃起來的感覺。

4.結論句（concluding sentence）：最後一句'Therefore, in a potluck meal, friends can not only get together but also enjoy great foods.'是結論句，重述主題句和朋友聚餐分享菜餚。

字彙與片語 ▶

英 文	詞 性	中 文
potluck	n.	每個人帶一道菜與大家分享的聚餐
dish	n.	菜餚
study abroad	v. phr.	到國外唸書
international	n.	國際的
Asian	n.	亞洲人
	adj.	亞洲的
Western	n.	西方的
sticky rice cakes	n. phr.	年糕
salty	adj.	鹹味的
flavor	n.	味道
elastic	adj.	有彈性的
chewy	adj.	有彈性的、黏著的
texture	n.	組織、質地
wonderful	n.	極好的、很棒的
cook	n.	廚師
curry chicken	n. phr.	咖哩雞
fill~with~	v. phr.	充滿
tiny	adj.	極小的
aroma	n.	香氣、香味
mixture	n.	混合
quiche	n.	法式奶蛋鹹派
recipe	n.	食譜
low-fat	adj.	低脂的

英　文	詞　性	中　文
ingredient	*adj.*	食材、原料
fiber-rich	*adj.*	富含纖維的
spinach	*n.*	菠菜
broccoli	*n.*	青花椰菜
cauliflower	*n.*	白花椰菜
mushroom	*n.*	蘑菇
tasty	*adj.*	美味的、可口的

文法解釋 ▶

❶ ~…each friend brings a different dish *shared* among a group of people.

　　　　　　名詞　　　　　　分詞片語作形容詞

　　分詞是具有形容詞的動詞形態，可以分為現在分詞（present participle）與過去分詞（past participle），兩者皆可修飾名詞，不過前者表示主動與進行的意思（例如：*The girl sitting in the car is my sister*），後者則表示被動的意義。分詞本身也具有動詞的性質，後面可接受詞、補語、副詞修飾它。在本句中，shared是過去分詞，'among a group of people'是副詞片語修飾過去分詞shared，兩者組成句法上的分詞片語，當作形容詞修飾前面的名詞dish。

　　另外，shared是過去分詞當形容詞用，可以改成關係形容詞子句的句型：

~…each friend brings a different dish which is *shared* among a group of people.

　　　　　　　　　　先行詞　　　　表限定之關係形容詞子句

❷ Most of my friends were from Asian countries..., *so that* we could taste foods....

從屬連接詞'... so that...'在本句中引導表示「結果」的副詞子句。此外它還可以引導表示「目的」的副詞子句。請看下面範例：

- I studied hard *so that* I could pass the examination.（目的）

我努力用功以便通過考試。

❸ I still remember the smell of curry *which* filled our tiny apartment with aroma.

先行詞　　　　表限定之關係形容詞子句

關係代名詞which前面沒有逗號，表示限定，且which具有代名詞的功用，替代「非人」的動物或無生物。which在本句中替代名詞詞組the smell of curry，做動詞filled的主詞。

❹ ~… it really *tasted* delicious.

動詞taste後面接形容詞的句型屬於我們前面提到「英語五大句型」中的第二種：S＋V＋SC（主詞+不完全不及物動詞+主詞補語）。這類動詞又稱為「連綴動詞」，後面接形容詞，語法上稱作補語，對主詞加以補充說明。此類動詞我們可以分成下幾種：

a. 表示狀態：be（是）、seem（似乎）。例如：

- He is busy. 他很忙。

b. 表示外在的樣子：look（看起來），appear（顯示出）。例如：

- She looks happy. 她看起來很高興。

c. 表示態度的保持：keep（繼續），remian（依然）。例如：

- She kept silent. 她保持沉默。

d. 表示感覺的感官動詞：taste（嚐起來），sound（聽起來），smell（聞起來），feel（感覺起來）。例如：

- That *sounds* ridiculous. 聽起來很荒謬。

- It *tastes* bitter. 吃起來苦苦的。

- It *smells* terrible. 聞起來很難聞。

- I *feel* sick. 我覺得不舒服。

e. 表示轉變：become（變成），get（漸漸變得），turn（變成）。例如：

- He is getting better. 他漸漸好起來。

❺ Her healthy quiche recipe included low-fat ingredients and fiber-rich vegetables *such as* spinach, broccoli and mushrooms.

'such as'意思等同於'for example'、'for instance'（例如；像是……），不過'such as'後面只接名詞或名詞詞組，不能接句子；'for example'、'for instance'可以接名詞、名詞詞組和句子。此外，'For example'、'For instance'後面若接句子時，不能用'such as'代替，本身視爲一個新的句子開始，第一個字母要大寫。請看下面範例：

- Tainan is famous for many historical monuments *such as* Confucius Temple and Anping Fort.

台南有許多出名的歷史古蹟像是孔廟和安平古堡。

- Tainan is famous for many historical monuments, *for example*, Confucius Temple and Anping Fort.

台南有許多出名的歷史古蹟，例如，孔廟和安平古堡。

- Tainan is famous for many historical monuments. *For example*, Confucius Temple is the oldest shrine in Taiwan.

台南有許多出名的歷史古蹟。例如,孔廟是台灣最古老的聖廟。

6 ~..., friends can *not only* get together *but also* enjoy great foods.

'... not only... but also ...'是累積式的對等連接詞,連接兩個語法層次相同的單字、片語或子句。若是連接兩個主詞時,重點在第二個主詞,動詞的單複數須與第二個主詞一致。例如:

- Not only you but also I am deceived by his appearance.

不只是你,連我也被他的外表騙了。

此外,also 也可以省略或放到句尾。Not only 亦可以置於句首,但是主詞與動詞或助動詞要倒裝。例如:

- In a potluck meal, friends can *not only* get together *but* enjoy great foods *also*.

- In a potluck meal, *not only* can friends get together *but also* enjoy great foods.

7 本範文裡單字Thai可以作名詞:泰國人,也可以當形容詞:泰國的,與一般表示國家人的詞尾不一樣。另外有些國家名稱與其對應的國家人拼寫方式完全不同。請比較下面範例:

Thailand(泰國)	Thai(*n.*泰國人)(*adj.*泰國的)
Taiwan(臺灣)	Taiwanese(*n.*臺灣人)(*adj.*臺灣的)
Japan(日本)	Japanese(*n.*日本人)(*adj.*日本的)
Korea(韓國)	Korean(*n.*韓國人)(*adj.*韓國的)
America(美國)	American(*n.*美國人)(*adj.*美國的)

France（法國）　　　　French（n.法國人）（adj.法國的）

Switzerland（瑞士）　　Swiss（n.瑞士人）（adj.瑞士的）

Sweden（瑞典）　　　　Swedish（n.瑞典人）（adj.瑞典的）

5. A Favorite Place from My Childhood

A favorite place from my childhood was Xiziwan, a natural bay located[1] in the west of Kaohsiung City. My parents used to[2] take us there to have some fun activities during school breaks. A tunnel served as the entrance to Xiziwan beach. I enjoyed[3] the cool breeze as I walked through the tunnel. The activities we usually had at the beach included riding inflatable rubber boat, building sand castles, and collecting shells[4]. Walking[5] along the coastal line, we could also watch the beautiful waves and some fishing boats. If it was a sunny day, the blue water and the clear sky presented a wonderful view. The view was particularly beautiful at sunset. In addition, we could take the ferry to Qijin, which is a peninsula to the south of Xiziwan. Now in my free time, I revisit Xiziwan beach and I become nostalgic as[6] it reminds me of the memories from the old days. The biggest[7] change is that many of the buildings and facilities have been modernized. The only one unchanged is that it remains an attractive tourist place. For all the above reasons, Xiziwan, in my memory, is a favorite childhood place.

童年最喜歡的地方

我童年最喜歡去的地方是西子灣，位於高雄西邊的一個天然海灣。學校放假期間，我的父母經常帶我們到那裡做一些有趣的活動。有一個隧道通到西子灣海灘的入口。我喜歡穿過隧道時吹來的涼爽微風。我們通常在沙灘上玩的活動包括乘坐充氣橡皮船、堆沙堡和撿貝殼。我們沿著海岸線也可以觀看美麗的浪花和一些漁船。如果是晴天，湛藍的海水和晴朗的天空呈現出一幅很漂亮的景色。特別是在日落的時候最美麗。此外，我們還可以搭乘渡輪到旗津，它是一個位在西子灣南邊的半島。現在，我有空的時候會到西子灣走走，有一種鄉愁的感覺，因為它讓我回憶起以前的記憶。我看到最大的變化是很多建築物和設施已經現代化。唯一不變的是，它仍然是一個很有吸引力的旅遊景點。基於上述原因，西子灣在我的記憶中是我童年最喜歡的地方。

段落結構 ▶

1.主題句（topic sentence）：第一句‘A favorite place from my childhood was Xiziwan, a natural bay located in the west of Kaohsiung City.’是主題句，指出作者童年最喜歡去的地方是西子灣。

2.支持句（supporting sentences）：介於主題句和結論句中間的句子都是支持句，介紹西子灣的風景和說明為什麼它是作者最喜歡去的地方。

3.結論句（concluding sentence）：最後一句‘For all the above reasons, Xiziwan, in my memory, is a favorite childhood place.’是結論句，與主題句相呼應。

4.描述性的段落（descriptive paragraphs）有客觀描寫及主觀描寫。本文除了客觀介紹西子灣的風景，還有作者主觀對這個童年最喜歡去的地方的感覺。

字彙與片語 ▶

英 文	詞 性	中 文
natural	*adj.*	天然的
bay	*n.*	海灣
be located	*v.*	位於、座落於
used to	*v. phr.*	過去時常、過去常做（但現在不會）
school break	*n. phr.*	學校不上課時、放假時
tunnel	*n.*	隧道
entrance	*n.*	入口
breeze	*n.*	微風、和風
ride	*v.*	乘坐

英　文	詞　性	中　文
inflatable	*adj.*	充氣的、膨脹的
rubber boat	*n.*	橡皮船
build	*v.*	建造
sand castles	*n.*	用沙堆起的城堡
collect	*v.*	收集、採集
shell	*n.*	貝殼
the coastal line	*n.*	海岸線
wave	*n.*	波浪
fishing boat	*n.*	捕魚船
clear sky	*n. phr.*	晴朗的天空
present	*v.*	呈現出
view	*n.*	視野
particularly	*adv.*	特別地、尤其
ferry	*n.*	渡輪
peninsula	*n.*	半島
nostalgic	*adj.*	鄉愁的
remind ~ of~	*v. phr.*	使想起
building	*n.*	建築物
facility	*n.*	設備、設施（複數facilities）
modernize	*v.*	使現代化
remain	*v.*	依然
attractive	*adj.*	吸引人的、引人注目的
tourist	*n.*	觀光客

文法解釋 ▶

❶ ~...Xiziwan, a natural bay <u>located in the west of Kaohsiung City</u>.

    名詞   分詞片語

本句是形容詞子句改爲「分詞片語」的用法，原句如下：

~...Xiziwan, a natural bay *which is* located in the west of Kaohsiung City.

    先行詞   關係形容詞子句

關係代名詞which與be動詞刪去後就成爲分詞片語，修飾前面的名詞 bay。要注意的是分詞片語在句法上只能做限定用，因此不可以用逗號分開。若可以用逗號分開的是「分詞構句」，句法上沒有限定的功用，它可能是形容詞子句或者是副詞子句簡化後用來補充説明句子裡的主詞。請比較下面範例：

 - The old man watching the TV ordered a beer. （分詞片語）

 = The old man who was watching the TV ordered a beer.

 那位看著電視的老人點了一瓶啤酒。

 - The old man, watching the TV, ordered a beer. （分詞構句）

 = Watching the TV, the old man ordered a beer.

 = As the old man was watching ther TV, he ordered a beer.

 那位老人，看著電視的時候，點了一瓶啤酒。

❷ My parents *used to* take us there to ~...

 請比較下面兩種句型：

 (1) 主詞＋used to＋原形動詞（過去的習慣，但目前已沒有）

- He used to play tennis every Sunday afternoon.

他以前習慣週日下午打網球。

(2) 主詞＋be used to＋動名詞（習慣於，目前仍持續）

- He is used to playing tennis every Sunday afternoon.

他習慣週日下午打網球。

❸ I *enjoyed* the cool breeze as I walked through the tunnel.

　　動詞'enjoy'後面只能接名詞或動名詞做受詞，不可以接不定詞to。例如：I *enjoyed walking* through the tunnel. 同樣的動詞還有mind（介意）、finish（完成）、quit（停止）、can't help（不得不）、resisit（抵抗）等等。

❹ The activities ..... included *riding* inflatable rubber boat, *building* sand castles and *collecting* shells.

　　本句中'riding'、'building'、'collecting'是動名詞，後面可以接受詞或補語等[2]。

(1) {riding^{Gerund} [(inflatable rubber)^{Adj} boat^{Noun}]$^{Dierect\ Object}$} $^{Noun\ group}$

(2) {building^{Gerund} [sand castles]$^{Direct\ Object}$} $^{Noun\ group}$

(3) [collecting^{Gerund} shells^{Noun}]$^{Noun\ group}$

　　我們以範例(1)為例做如下說明：'inflatable rubber'是兩個形容詞同時修飾後面的名詞boat；'inflatable rubber boat'句法上是當動名詞riding的直接受詞；這一串字'riding inflatable rubber boat'組成名詞詞組，做整個句子裡動詞included的直接受詞。

---

[2] 名詞解釋：Gerund（動名詞）；Noun（名詞）；Noun group（名詞詞組）；Adj= Adjective（形容詞）；Direct Object（直接受詞）。

❺ Walking along the coastal line, we could also watch the beautiful waves and some fishing boats.

本句為分詞片語，也可寫成As we walked along the coastal line, we could also watch the beautiful waves and some fishing boats.

❻ ~... I become nostalgic *as* it reminds me of the memories from the old days.

表原因的從屬子句

'as' 在此句裡表示原因的連接詞，其所引導的子句可以放在主要子句之前，也可以放在主要子句的後面。例如：

- *As I am sick*, I cannot go to the movies with you.

因為我生病了，我不能跟你去看電影。

- You should serve him first as he is the oldest.

你應該先為他服務，因為他是最年長的。

❼ *The biggest change* is that many of the buildings and facilities have

主詞   　　　　　that + 子句 = 主詞補語

been modernized.

'biggest ['bɪgɪst]' 是形容詞原級 'big [bɪg]' 的最高級。從構詞學來看，單音節的形容詞最後一個字母是子音，且這個子音緊跟在短母音的後面，這時候它的比較級與最高級必須先重複字尾的子音，然後再加上-er, -est。例如：

big	bigger	biggest
hot	hotter	hottest
fat	fatter	fattest

本範文中用最高級形容詞表達最好、最優的結構如下：

... + the + 形容詞最高級 + 單數名詞 + be + that + 子句

'The biggest change' 做主詞，be動詞後面接連接詞that引導的子句當主詞補語。

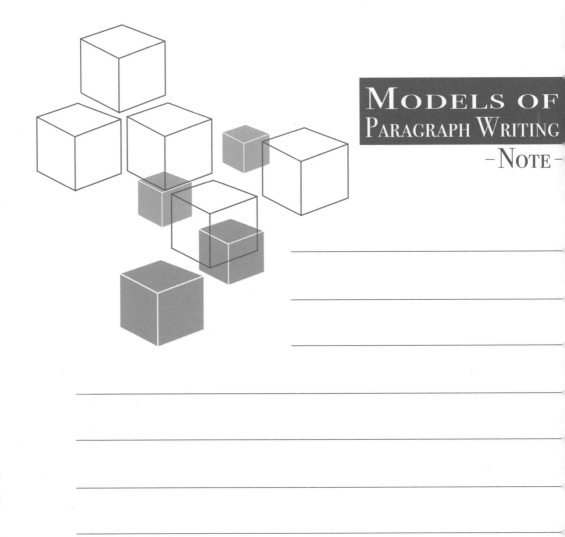

MODELS OF
PARAGRAPH WRITING
-NOTE-

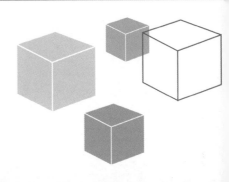

記敘性的段落
NARRATIVE PARAGRAPHS

　　記敘性的段落文體就是說故事，它好比一個舞台劇，分成好幾個場景，逐一講述故事、劇情發生的經過。敘述性段落有以下幾點特色：

1. 記敘性段落通常有一個開頭（beginning）、經過（middle）、和結尾（end）。

2. 記敘性段落會按照時間先後順序來敘述故事，用表達時間的字詞做連接，如：first、before、after、when、during、finally。

3. 記敘性段落通常用過去式來敘述事情的發生經過。

4. 記敘性段落可以用第一人稱（I或we）來敘述，也可用第三人稱（he, she, they）來敘述。

　　記敘性段落（narrative paragraphs）主要在說明「誰（who）」、「什麼時候（when）」、「什麼地方（where）」、「發生了什麼事（what）」。與描述性段落（descriptive paragraphs）不同的是記敘性段落著重於說明動作發生的經過、方式，好像是偵探在調查解釋一個事件。描述性段落則強調人、物或景色的外表讓我們的感官有什麼樣的感覺。以下是記敘性的段落文體我們提供的五篇範文。

第一篇文章 My English learning experiences 敘述英語學習的經驗

第二篇文章 An unforgettable trip 敘述一次難忘的旅行

第三篇文章 A travel nightmare 敘述一次不愉快的旅遊經驗

第四篇文章 The most frightening experience 敘述最可怕的經驗

第五篇文章 My first time to be a receptionist 敘述第一次擔任接待員的經驗

1. My English Learning Experiences

My English learning experiences can be divided into three periods. When I was a fifth grader, my parents sent me to a children English cram school where[1] I started learning English in an interesting way. We learned vocabulary and conversation through interactive activities and I loved to listen to the teacher telling fairy stories[2]. The teacher gave us candies and stickers as rewards if we performed well in English[3]. During my junior high school years, English became a subject to master instead of a language for communication in the real world. English learning was no longer fun. The teacher was an authority in the classroom and the teaching was test-oriented. In order to[4] pass the high school entrance exam, we did a lot of drill practices and translation of English sentences into Chinese and vice versa. Even though[5] the English classes were boring in junior high school, my performance in English surpassed the other students. Unfortunately when I entered in senior high school, I faced my first bottleneck. The English materials seemed much more[6] difficult than those in junior high school, and I had many competitors in class. I never gave up but studied harder. Finally, I regained my interest and confidence in learning English. Now I am an English major student in college, and I make up my mind to become an English teacher in the future.

我的英語學習經驗

　　我的英語學習過程可分為三個階段。在我五年級的時候，我的父母把我送到兒童美語補習班，那裡剛開始英語學習的方式是有趣的。老師藉由互動的遊戲來讓我們學習詞彙和對話，我也喜歡聽老師講童話故事。如果我們英語表現好的話，老師會給我們糖果和貼紙作為獎勵。到了國中後，英語變成一個科目，而不是在生活上用來溝通的語言。英語學習不再有樂趣。課堂上老師代表權威，而且教學方式是考試取向的。為了通過高中入學考，我們做了很多句型練習，還有英翻中和中翻英的練習。即使國中的英語課很無趣，我的英語成績超越其他同學。遺憾的是，當我進入高中後，我遇到了我的第一個瓶頸。高中的英語教材比國中的似乎更加困難了，我在課堂上也多了許多競爭對手。但我從未放棄，而是更加用功。最後，我重拾學習英語的興趣和信心。現在，我是一位主修英語的大學生，我下定決心未來要成為一位英語教師。

段落結構 ▶

　　1.主題句（topic sentence）：第一句'My English learning experiences can be divided into three periods.'是主題句，作者把她的英語學習過程分為三個階段。

　　2.支持句（supporting sentences）：介於主題句和結論句中間的句子都是支持句，分為三個階段：兒童美語補習班的學習是有趣的，國中時期的學習是以考試為取向，高中時遇到瓶頸但最後重拾學習英語的興趣和信心。

　　3.結論句（concluding sentence）：最後一句'I make up my mind to become an English teacher in the future.'是結論句。

字彙與片語 ▶

英　文	詞　性	中　文
grader	n.	～年級學生
cram school	n.	補習班
vocabulary	n.	字彙
conversation	n.	會話
interactive	adj.	互動的
fairy stories	n.	童話故事
sticker	n.	貼紙
reward	n.	獎勵
perform	n.	表現
subject	n.	科目
master	v.	精通
instead of	prep. phr.	而不是
communication	n.	溝通
no longer	adv.	不再
authority	n.	權威
test-oriented	adj.	考試取向的
entrance exam	n.	入學考試
drill	n.	重複不斷的練習
vice versa	n.	反之亦然
surpass	n.	優於、勝過
unfortunately	adv.	不幸地
bottleneck	n.	瓶頸
competitor	n.	競爭者

英　文	詞　性	中　文
regain	*n.*	恢復
make up one's mind	*v. phr.*	下定決心
in the future	*prep. phr.*	未來

文法解釋▶

❶ ~... my parents sent me to a <u>children English cram school</u> *where* I <u>started learning English *in* an interesting way.</u>

　　'where'是關係副詞，用於表示地方的名詞（亦即children English cram school）之後，引導形容詞子句（本句虛線的部份）。補充說明的是：關係副詞所引導的是形容詞子句，疑問副詞所引導的是名詞子句。請比較下面兩句：

　　- The street <u>where he lives</u> is near my house.
　　　　　關係副詞引導形容詞子句
　　他住的街離我家很近。

　　- Do you know <u>where he lives</u>?
　　　　　疑問副詞引導名詞子句
　　你知道他住哪裡嗎？

❷ ~··· I loved to listen to the teacher *telling* fairy stories.
　　tell, talk, say, speak的意思都是「說」，但用法不同：
　　tell：tell a story（說故事），tell the truth（說實話）
　　talk：talk to 人（向人說話），talk about事（談論事情）

speak：speak + 語言，speak English

say：She said that she was sick.（她說她生病了）

It is said that + 子句 = People say that + 子句（據説⋯）

❸ The teacher gave us candies as rewards *if* we performed well in English.

首先，本句是直説法的條件句，也就是説，句中所敘述的是客觀的事實，發生在過去。因此if引導的條件句其動詞語態用陳述式，而不是假設語態的動詞。其次，as在本句是作介系詞用，意思是「擔任」、「當作」。

❹ *In order to* pass the high school entrance exam, we did a lot of drill practices ~⋯

'in order to'是表目的之不定詞片語，當主要子句的主詞和副詞子句的主詞相同時，可用此不定詞片語的句型；或是用in order that從屬連接詞的句子結構，原句可寫成如下：

- We did a lot of drill practices ~... *in order that* we could pass the high school entrance exam.'

❺ *Even though* the English classes were boring in junior high school, my performance in English surpassed *the other* students.

'Even though'為從屬連接詞，在本句可用'Although'或'Though'代替。

❻ The English materials seemed much *more* difficult *than* those in junior high school, and ~⋯

形容詞的比較結構如下：~ V + *more* + Adj. + *than* + ~. 比較級之前不可用very修飾，而是用程度副詞much、far、a great deal或a little修飾。此外不可

以弄錯比較對象，有時會造成意義不同，有時候則是語法上的錯誤。請看下面範例：

- I like you better than <u>she</u> (likes you).

我喜歡你勝於她（喜歡你）＝我比她更喜歡你。

➡ 本句是兩個主詞：I和she的比較。

- I like you better than her. ＝ I like you better than (I like) her.

我喜歡你勝於我喜歡她＝我比較喜歡你，而不是她。

➡ 本句是兩個受詞：you和her的比較。

- *The weather of Singapore is hotter than Taiwan.

此句的錯誤在於比較對象：不應該把the weather of Singapore拿來和Taiwan做比較。正確的說法如下：

- The weather of Singapore is hotter than *that of* Taiwan.

➡ 'that'是the weather的代名詞。

2. An Unforgettable Trip

I had a memorable skiing experience when I was studying in the United States. During one winter break, some friends and I went skiing in Lake Tahoe, a ski resort located along the border between California and Nevada. I was so excited that[1] I could not sleep during the night before heading for Lake Tahoe. We arrived at the ski resort in the afternoon and stayed at a cabin. The next morning, we rented the skiing equipments and the ski coach taught us the basics of skiing including how to turn and how to stop. After practicing[2] the basic skills, we rode the ski lift to the top of the snowy hill. There were

three levels of ski slopes, each of which[3] was marked by a different color: green trail for beginners, blue trail for intermediate skiers, and black trail for expert skiers. We chose the green trail since we were all beginners. As[4] we skied down, it was thrilling but scary because I found I could not stop but[5] keep on sliding down. Suddenly, I lost my balance and fell down with my body buried inside the snow. I managed to use my ski pole to stand up with my friends' help. If[6] I came into someone's way, I made myself fall to the ground to avoid accidents. We spent three days in Lake Tahoe. This was an unforgettable trip and I hope I will go skiing[7] again one day.

難忘的旅行

我在美國留學時有一次難忘的滑雪經驗。一個寒假期間,我和幾個朋友去太浩湖滑雪,它是一個位於美國加州和內華達州之間的滑雪勝地。在前往太浩湖的前一天晚上,我興奮地睡不著。我們在下午時到達滑雪勝地,住在一間小木屋。第二天早上,我們租用滑雪設備,有滑雪教練教我們滑雪的基本技巧,包括如何轉彎以及如何停下來。我們練習這些技巧後,乘坐滑雪纜車到山頂。滑雪道有三個級別,不同的顏色代表不同的級別:綠色為初級滑雪道,藍色為中級滑雪道,黑色為高級滑雪道。我們選擇了綠色滑雪道,因為我們都是初學者。開始滑下去時很刺激但也很可怕,因為我發現我沒辦法停下來而一直往下滑。突然間,我失去平衡摔倒了,我的身體埋在雪裡面。我試著用我的雪杖,在我朋友的協助下站起來。如果遇到前面有人來不及停下來,我會故意摔倒在地,以避免發生意外。我們在太浩湖待了三天。這是一個難忘的旅程,我希望以後還有機會去滑雪。

段落結構 ▶

1.主題句(topic sentence):第一句'I had a memorable skiing experience when I was studying in the United States.'是主題句,點出作者在美國留學時有一次難忘的滑雪經驗。

2.支持句(supporting sentences):介於主題句和結論句中間的句子都是支持句,敘述在太浩湖滑雪的經過。

3.結論句(concluding sentence):最後一句'This was an unforgettable trip and I hope I will go skiing again one day.'是結論句,呼應主題句,再次強調此次旅行令人難忘。

字彙與片語 ▶

英　文	詞　性	中　文
memorable	adj.	難忘的
winter break	n.	寒假
ski resort	n.	滑雪勝地
border	n.	邊界、邊境
cabin	n.	小木屋
rent	v.	租用
equipments	n.	裝備
ski coach	n.	滑雪教練
basics	n.	基礎、基本技巧
ride	v.	乘坐（動詞三態ride, rode, ridden）
ski lift	n.	滑雪纜車
snowy hill	n.	雪覆蓋的山坡地
ski slope	n.	滑雪坡
mark	v.	標記
trail	n.	小道
intermediate	adj.	中級程度的
skier	n.	滑雪的人
expert	n.	專家、熟練者
thrilling	adj.	刺激的
scary	adj.	可怕的
slide down	v.	滑下
suddenly	adv.	突然地
lose my balance	v. phr.	失去平衡（動詞三態lose, lost, lost）

英　文	詞　性	中　文
fall down	*v.*	跌倒（動詞三態fall, fell, fallen）
bury	*v.*	埋藏
manage	*v.*	設法做到
ski pole	*n.*	滑雪杖
fall to the ground	*v. phr.*	摔倒在地
accident	*n.*	意外
unforgettable	*adj.*	難忘的

文法解釋▶

❶ I was *so* excited *that* I could not sleep during the night before *heading* for Lake Tahoe.

　　首先，so...that（如此…以致於）表示結果的從屬連接詞，so是副詞，後面接形容詞。that引導表示結果的副詞子句，與前面表原因的「so + 形容詞」呼應。其次，before heading for Lake Tahoe = before I headed for Lake Tahoe。

❷ After practicing the basic skills, we rode the ski lift to the top of the snowy hill.
　　　　從屬子句　　　　　　　　　　　　　　主要子句

　　After為表時間的從屬連接詞，連接主要子句和從屬子句。After practicing the basic skills = After we practiced the basic skills 若兩個子句的主詞相同，從屬子句裡的主詞we可以省略，但動詞practiced必須改成動名詞practicing。

　　如果主要子句和從屬子句的主詞不同時，兩個子句的主詞都必須保

留。例如：

After the coach taught us the basic skills, we rode the ski lift to the top of the snowy hill. 這時候就不能改成After teaching us the basic skills, we rode the ski lift to the top of the snowy hill.

❸ There were three levels of ski slopes, *each of which* was marked by a different color: ~...

關係代名詞which通常緊跟著先行詞（three levels of ski slopes）的後面，但有時候語意上的需要可插入其它的字：each of which表示「三個級別」（three levels ~）裡的每一項，句法上是單數，因此後面接單數動詞。

❹ *As* we skied down, it was thrilling *but* scary because I found I could not stop but keep on sliding down.

首先，'as'是表示時間的從屬連接詞，語意上與when或while不同的是'as'強調連接的兩個動作、狀態是逐漸發展或演變。例如，下面的範例用when或while連接詞就不適合。

- We are getting more mature *as* we advance in years.

隨著年歲的增長，我們變得更成熟。

❺ I found I could not stop but *keep on* sliding down.

「keep on（繼續）」是一動詞片語後面接動名詞。

❻ *If* I came into someone's way, I made myself fall to the ground to avoid accidents.

'if'是表示條件的從屬連接詞，本句中所敘述的是過去的事實，動詞語態用陳述式（直說法），而不是假設語態的動詞。

❼ I will *go skiing* again one day.

本句中，go是完全不及物動詞，後面接動名詞，表示去從事某種活動。

3. A Travel Nightmare

A travel nightmare occurred during my first trip to China. Several years ago, our family joined a tour to Jiuzhaigou Valley, which was known for the fabulous scenery like[1] multi-level waterfalls and colorful lakes. However, I was shocked at the serious social problems. When we arrived at a small village the day before entering Jiuzhaigou Valley, I was surprised to see many children beggars on the street. A group of children in old and shabby clothes approached and surrounded us, asking us to buy postcards and souvenirs. Some even asked for money. We were told by the tour guide not to give money to beggars since[2] some were pickpockets. It was said that these children were trained to become beggars by[3] a criminal gang. They were unable to escape from this miserable situation. Then, what[4] happened next irritated me. A couple of peddlers touted their juicy fruits. After picking some good pears and paying the money, we found what[5] we got were all rotten ones[6]. We understood that we were cheated. It was useless to[7] argue with the peddler because he never admitted[8] deceiving our money. This was an unpleasant experience. I felt sympathetic for the children beggars but was upset about the greedy culture.

旅遊夢魘

　　這個旅遊夢魘發生在我第一次到中國旅行的時候。多年前，我們全家參加旅行團到九寨溝，它是個以美麗風景聞名的地方，有多層次的瀑布和五彩繽紛的湖泊。不過，讓我驚訝的是內地嚴重的社會問題。在我們進入九寨溝的前一天，我們來到一個小村莊，我很驚訝地看到許多兒童在街頭乞討。一群孩子穿著破舊的衣服上前包圍了我們，要求我們買明信片和紀念品，有些甚至直接要錢。導遊告訴我們不要拿錢給這些兒童乞丐，因為有些是扒手。據說這些孩子被犯罪集團控制訓練成為要錢的乞丐，他們無法逃離這個悲慘的情況。然後，接下來發生的事令我惱怒。有一些小販推銷兜售水果，在我們挑選一些好的梨子並付錢之後，我們發現拿到的都是爛的梨子。我們知道被騙了。但是與小販爭辯是沒有用的，因為他從不承認騙了我們的錢。這是一個不愉快的經驗。我同情那些兒童乞丐，但也對貪婪的文化感到生氣。

段落結構 ▶

　　1.主題句（topic sentence）：第一句'A travel nightmare occurred during my first trip to China.'是主題句，點出作者到中國旅行遇到一些不愉快的經驗。

　　2.支持句（supporting sentences）：介於主題句和結論句中間的句子都是支持句，敘述在中國旅行的經過，看到許多兒童在街頭乞討和買水果被騙。

　　3.結論句（concluding sentence）：最後兩句'This was an unpleasant experience. I felt sympathetic for the children beggars but was upset about the greedy culture.'是結論句，表達作者對此次旅行的感覺。

字彙與片語 ▶

英　文	詞　性	中　文
nightmare	*n.*	夢魘
occur	*v.*	發生
Jiuzhaigou Valley	*n.*	九寨溝（也叫做Nine Village Valley）
irritate = annoy	*v.*	使生氣、惱怒
annoy = irritate	*v.*	使生氣、惱怒
deceive = cheat	*v.*	欺騙
tour	*n.*	旅遊、旅行
was known for	*v. phr.*	以～聞名
fabulous	*adj.*	極好的
scenery	*n.*	風景
waterfall	*n.*	瀑布
colorful	*adj.*	五彩繽紛的
arrive	*v.*	到達
beggar	*n.*	乞丐
shabby	*v.*	破爛的
approach	*v.*	接近
surround	*v.*	圍繞
postcard	*n.*	明信片
souvenir	*n.*	紀念品
tour guide	*n.*	導遊
it is said that~	*clause*	據說
pickpocket	*n.*	扒手
criminal gang	*n.*	犯罪集團

英　文	詞　性	中　文
escape	*v.*	逃離
miserable	*adj.*	悲慘的
a couple of	*prep. phr.*	數個
peddler	*n.*	小販
tout	*v.*	兜售
juicy	*adj.*	多汁的
rotten	*adj.*	腐爛的
argue with	*v. phr.*	和～爭吵
admit	*v.*	承認
unpleasant	*adj.*	不愉快的
sympathetic	*adj.*	有同情心的
upset	*adj.*	生氣的
greedy	*adj.*	貪婪的

文法解釋▶

❶ Jiuzhaigou was known for the fabulous scenery *like* multi-level waterfalls and colorful lakes.

　　like = such as

　　另外，補充such…as（像…這樣）的用法：

　　句法上，like是介系詞後面接受格，as是作補語的關係代名詞，後面接的形容詞子句可省略，只保留作為主詞的名詞或代名詞。請看下列範例：

　　- I have never seen such a great tennis player as he (is).

　　= I have never seen such a great tennis player like him.

　　我從未見過像他這樣偉大的網球選手。

❷ We were told by the tour guide not to give money to beggars *since* some were pickpockets.

　　*Since*是表示原因的從屬連接詞，語氣比because弱，但比as稍強。

❸ It was said that these children were trained to become beggars *by* a criminal gang.

　　本句中介系詞by作被動語態中的施事者，表示「被～」的意思。

❹ *What* happened next irritated me.

　　本句中what本身是兼做先行詞的關係代名詞，引導名詞子句做動詞irritated的主詞。What = the thing that或the thing which。

　　<u>What happened next</u> irritated me.
　　名詞子句作主詞

❺ ~... we found *what* we got were all rotten ones.

　　本句中what是複合關係代名詞，引導名詞子句做動詞found的受詞。What = 先行詞 + 關係代名詞（*the thing that*或*the thing which*）。

　　- We found <u>*what* we got</u> were all rotten ones.
　　　　　　名詞子句

❻ ~... we found what we got were all rotten *ones*.

　　本句中ones代替複數名詞pears。

❼ *It was useless to* argue *with* the peddler ~...

　　*It*是虛主詞或形式上的主詞代替本句後面所要說的不定詞。換句話說，不定詞片語才是真正的主詞。

　　It was useless to argue with the peddler ~...
　　虛主詞　　　　　　　真正的主詞

　　本句中介系詞with與動詞argue連用，表示「反對」、「不一致」的意思。其它類似的動詞片語我們列舉如下：
- to battle with 　　　　與～搏鬥
- to fight with 　　　　　與～打鬥
- to compete with 　　　與～競爭
- to cope with 　　　　　應付
- to debate with 　　　　與～爭論

❽ ~... he never *admitted* deceiving our money.

　　本句中動詞admit後面只可接動名詞為受詞，不可接不定詞。

　　其它同樣後面接動名詞的動詞如下：

- avoid	避免	- deny	否認
- enjoy	享受、喜歡	- mind	介意、反對
- finish	完成	- resist	抵抗
- quit	停止	- consider	考慮
- escape	逃避	- can't help	不得不

4. The Most Frightening Experience

The most[1] frightening experience happened when I lost control of my car on the highway in the United States. In the first semester of my study abroad, I lived in a house whose owner was a Taiwanese immigrant, and he rented out the rooms to students. With[2] the help of my landlord, I bought a used car because the house was not on the school shuttle route. It was a twenty-minute drive[3] from where I lived to the university. On a rainy day while I was driving back from school, my car skidded on the wet road. I slammed on the brakes but could not stop the car. I tried to pull my car over to the shoulder but it was not under my control. I was afraid that my car might turn over. Fortunately, my car finally stopped on the shoulder of the highway. I was lucky that no car hit from behind, which[4] would otherwise cause a car accident. At that time, I did not have a cell phone to call for help. I still drove slowly home. The next morning, I went to the auto shop and the technician told me that both of the rear tires of my car were worn out. Then I realized that the car dealer was not honest when I bought the car. He should have changed[5] the tires before selling the car to me. I learned from this experience that I needed to have a pre-purchase inspection done[6] before buying a car.

最可怕的經驗

　　我最可怕的經歷是有一次我的車在美國高速公路上失去了控制。在我出國念書的第一個學期,我住的房子的主人是一位台灣移民過來的人,他把家裡的房間租給學生。在房東的協助下,我買了一輛二手車,因為我住的地方沒有學校公車可搭。從我住的地方到學校約20分鐘的車程。在一個下雨天,當我開車從學校回來時,車子在潮濕的路面上打滑。我猛踩剎車,但無法讓車子停下來。我試著把車子開到路肩,但我的車失去了控制。我很害怕我會翻車。幸運的是,我的車最後終於在路肩上停下來。還好後面沒有車過來,否則會導致車禍。當時我沒有手機打電話求救。我還是慢慢地開回家。隔天早上,我去汽車修理店,技術人員告訴我車子的兩個後輪已經磨平了。這時我才知道,賣車給我的商人是不老實的。把車子給我之前,他應該先把磨損的輪胎換掉。從這經驗我學到在買車前要先請人做檢查。

段落結構 ▶

1.主題句（topic sentence）：第一句'The most frightening experience happened when I lost control of my car on the highway in the United States.'是主題句，點出作者在美國高速公路上車子失控的可怕經驗。

2.支持句（supporting sentences）：介於主題句和結論句中間的句子都是支持句，可分爲三個階段：買了二手車，在高速公路上車子打滑失去控制，最後發現車子後輪已磨平。

3.結論句（concluding sentence）：最後一句'I learned from this experience that I needed to have a pre-purchase inspection done before buying a car.'是結論句，說明作者從這次事件中學到的經驗。

字彙與片語 ▶

英　文	詞　性	中　文
frightening	*adj.*	可怕的
lose control of	*v. phr.*	失去控制（動詞三態lose, lost, lost）
highway	*n.*	高速公路
immigrant	*n.*	移民者
rent out	*v.*	出租
landlord	*n.*	房東
used car	*n.*	二手車
school shuttle	*n.*	校車
route	*n.*	路線
drive	*n.*	車程
skid	*v.*	打滑（動詞三態skid, skidded, skidded）

英　文	詞　性	中　文
slam	*v.*	猛踩（動詞三態slam, slammed, slammed）
brake	*n.*	剎車
pull (my car) over	*v. phr.*	把（我的車）開到路邊
shoulder	*n.*	路肩
turn over	*v.*	翻車
hit from behind	*v. phr.*	從後面撞擊
otherwise	*adv.*	否則
auto shop	*n.*	汽車修理店
technician	*n.*	技術人員
rear	*adj.*	後面的
be worn out	*v. phr.*	磨光的
realize	*v.*	了解
dealer	*n.*	經銷商
honest	*adj.*	誠實的
pre-purchase	*n.*	購買前
inspection	*n.*	檢查

文法解釋 ▶

❶ The most frightening experience happened ～…

　　如果形容詞是兩個或三個以上的音節所組成的單字，或者字尾是-ful、-able、-ive、-ing等，其比較級與最高級是在形容詞原級的前面加上more和most。例如：

important	*more* important	*most* important
beautiful	*more* beautiful	*most* beautiful
interesting	*more* interesting	*most* interesting
diligent	*more* diligent	*most* diligent
courteous	*more* courteous	*most* courteous

以下我們再列舉出形容詞最高級的表達方式：

(1) ...＋the＋形容詞最高級＋單數名詞＋of/among＋人或物（複數形）

   - He is the most diligent boy among them.

   他是他們之中最勤奮的孩子。

(2) ...＋the＋形容詞最高級＋單數名詞＋that＋子句

   - She is the best cook that I have ever heard.

   她是我聽過最好的廚師。

(3) ... one of＋the＋形容詞最高級＋複數名詞＋that …

   - Mozart was one of the greatest musicians that ever lived.

   莫札特是世界上最偉大的音樂家之一。

❷ With the help of my landlord, I bought a used car ～…

   With the help of my landlord為介系詞片語的用法，此句等於My landlord helped me to buy a used car.

❸ It was a *twenty-minute drive* from where I lived to the university.

   'a twenty-minute drive' 其中的twenty-minute是名詞作形容詞來表示單位，修飾後面的名詞，仍用單數形式。請看下面範例：

a five-year-old boy 　　　　一個五歲大男孩

a fifteen-story building　　一棟十五層樓高的建築

❹ I was lucky that no car hit from behind, *which* would otherwise cause a
car accident.　　　　主要子句（先行詞）

　'which'是關係代名詞作主詞用，代替前面整個子句，或者說先行詞就
是前面整個子句。

❺ He *should have changed* the tires before selling the car to me.

　在'should have + Vpp'的句型中，說話者認為有「難以相信，該做而未
做，或不應該如此」的意思。should是假設語氣的用法，表達主觀意念，非
客觀事實。

❻ I needed to *have* a pre-purchase inspection *done* before buying a car.

　'have + 受詞 + 過去分詞'的句型表示「被動經驗和使役」，have是使役
動詞，done後面的受詞（by someone）省略掉。請再看下面範例：

　- I had my car repaired.

　我拿我的車去修理。

　另外，get和make也當使役動詞。

　「get + 受詞 + 過去分詞」

　- I got my tires changed.

　我（請人）把我的輪胎換掉。

　「make + 受詞 + 過去分詞」

　- I try to make myself understood when communicating with foreigners.

　當我和外國人溝通時，我試著讓對方了解我講的英文。

5. My First Time to Be a Receptionist

My first time to be^❶ a receptionist was an interesting experience. In my junior year in college, the Asian boxing competition took place in Kaohsiung and the boxing association recruited English major students as part time receptionists and interpreters. Our job was to receive the boxers and coaches during their stay in Kaohsiung. My first contact with the Sri Lanka coach was on the way back from the competition site to the hotel. We sat together on the bus. After greeting and shaking hands with each other, we started to chat. I had a hard time understanding what^❷ he said because he pronounced some words differently. For example, /t/ was pronounced as^❸ /d/ and /w/ as /v/. Because of the accent, I misunderstood what he meant. When he said "little," I thought that he said "leader." This turned out to be an awkward situation. He also used some words differently. He said, "I was here three years back" instead of "I was here three years ago." On the last day, he asked me to accompany him to buy Chinese handicrafts. Then I was an interpreter for him and the businessman. I was delighted that I helped both sides compromise at^❹ a reasonable price. From this experience, I learned that American English was not the only variety of English^❺ and I should get accustomed to different accents of spoken English around the world.

第一次擔任接待員

我第一次擔任接待員是個有趣的經驗。在我大三那年,亞洲拳擊比賽在高雄舉行,拳擊協會催用英語主修的學生擔任接待員和翻譯人員。我們的工作是接待拳擊手和教練。我第一次與斯里蘭卡教練接觸是從比賽現場回到旅館的路上。我們在公車上坐隔壁,與對方問候和握手後,我們開始聊天。我發現很難理解他說的英語,因為他的發音不太一樣,例如,/t/發成/d/而/w/發成/v/。因為口音的關係,我誤解他的意思。當他說「小」這個字,我以為他是說「領導者」,這造成一個尷尬的場面。還有他使用的字不太一樣,他說,「三年前我來過這裡」,他說three years back而不是three years ago。最後一天,他要我陪他去買中國手工藝品,那時我成為他和商人的翻譯人員。我很高興我幫雙方協調一個合理的價格。從這經驗中,我學到美式英語不是唯一的英語種類,我應該學習去習慣世界各地不同的英語口音。

段落結構 ▶

1.主題句（topic sentence）：第一句'My first time to be a receptionist in my junior year was an interesting experience.'是主題句，點出作者第一次擔任接待員是個有趣的經驗。

2.支持句（supporting sentences）：介於主題句和結論句中間的句子都是支持句，敘述接待斯里蘭卡教練的經過。

3.結論句（concluding sentence）：最後一句'From this experience, I learned that American English was not the only variety of English and I should get accustomed to different accents of spoken English around the world.'是結論句，說明作者從這次經驗中學到不同地區的英語有不同的口音。

字彙與片語 ▶

英　文	詞　性	中　文
receptionist	*n.*	接待員
junior	*n.*	大三生
	adj.	大三的（四年制大學）
boxing	*n.*	拳擊
competition	*n.*	比賽
take place	*v.*	舉行
association	*n.*	協會
recruit	*v.*	招收新成員
interpreter	*n.*	口譯員
receive	*v.*	接待
boxer	*n.*	拳擊手

英　文	詞　性	中　文
coach	*n.*	教練
contact	*n.*	接觸
on the way	*adv.*	在～路上
site	*n.*	地點、場所
have a hard time	*v. phr.*	遇到困難
pronounce	*v.*	發音
accent	*n.*	口音
misunderstand	*v.*	誤解
turn out to	*v. phr.*	變成
awkward	*adj.*	尷尬的
accompany	*v.*	陪伴
handicraft	*n.*	手工藝品
delighted	*adj.*	高興的
compromise	*v.*	妥協
reasonable	*adj.*	合理的
variety	*n.*	種類
get accustomed to	*v. phr.*	習慣於

文法解釋▶

❶ {[My first time *to be* a receptionist]主詞 was [an interesting experience]述語}句子.
　　　名詞詞組　　　形容詞

　　'to be'是不定詞，其特點是具有名詞、形容詞和副詞的動詞形態，用來表示動作。本句中'to be a receptionist'是當形容詞用，置於所修飾的名詞或名詞詞組後面，句法上是限定的用法。

以下我們舉例不定詞名詞和副詞的用法：

- *To err* is human, *to forgive* divine.　　〔名詞作主詞〕

犯錯是人，寬恕是神。

- The worst is still *to come*.　　〔名詞作主詞補語〕

最糟的還在後面。

- We eat *to live*, not live *to eat*.　　〔作副詞用修飾動詞表目的〕

我們吃飯是爲了活著，不是活著爲了吃飯。

- This sofa is comfortable *to sit on*.　　〔作副詞用修飾形容詞〕

這沙發坐起來很舒服。

❷ I had a hard time understanding *what* he said ～…

　　本句中what本身兼作先行詞的關係代名詞，引導名詞子句作動詞 understanding的受詞。What等於「先行詞＋關係代名詞」（*the thing that*或 *the thing which*），有時也作all that的意思。

- I don't know what you really want.

　　　　the thing which

我不知道你眞正要什麼。

　　另外had a hard time後面接動名詞其實是前面省略了介系詞in亦即：'I had a hard time in understanding ～'.

❸ For example, /t/ was pronounced *as* /d/ and /w/ *as* /v/.

　　as在本句是介系詞，意思是「如同」、「像」。/w/ was pronounced as /v/. 其中was pronounced重覆所以省略。請再看下面例句：

- He treats me *as* his child.

= He treats me *as if I were* his child.

他待我如同他的孩子一般。

❹ I helped both sides compromise *at* a reasonable price.

介系詞at表示「以～的價格」、「以～的代價」。

- All success must be bought at the price of pain and sacrifice.

所有的成功都要以痛苦和犧牲付出代價。

❺ American English was not the only variety of English.

世界上不同地區的英語有其不同特性，在發音、用字遣詞上不太一樣，因此有所謂的美式（American English）、英式（British English）、澳洲（Australian English）、加拿大（Canadian English）、印度（Indian English）、南非（South African English）等等不同的英語。

表達意見的段落
OPINION PARAGRAPHS

　　陳述意見的段落表達，作者必須對某個主題提出自己的觀點和意見，贊成或不贊成的原因是什麼，說明理由並舉例支持看法。避免使用迂迴的方式敘述，而是明確、清楚地說出。表達意見的段落有以下幾點特色：

1. 作者陳述對某個主題的意見。

2. 除了作者的觀點，也要用事實來支持論點。

3. 通常是對有爭議性的議題（controversial issue）提出看法。

4. 啟發讀者思考對此議題的看法。

5. 最後用一兩句來反駁相反的意見（counter-argument）。

6. 表達支持的字和片語有agree with, support, advocate, be in favor of…等。

7. 表達反對的字和片語有disagree with, oppose, object to…等。

以下是表達意見的段落我們提供的五篇範文：

第一篇文章 Bilingual education for children 對兒童雙語教育的看法

第二篇文章 Cosmetic surgery 對整容手術的看法

第三篇文章 The use of cell phone in public places
　　　　　　在公共場所使用手機的看法

第四篇文章 Lotteries 對樂透彩券的看法

第五篇文章 If I were the mayor 如果我是市長我會怎麼做

1. Bilingual Education for Children

I am in favor of bilingual education for children for a number of reasons. First, children are more likely to acquire authentic pronunciation than adults[1]. The early years of life are the critical period, in which[2] an individual can acquire a native-like accent. In addition, the research results show that bilingual children are able to distinguish and pronounce certain sounds which do not exist in their first language, while[3] adult learners may lack this ability. Some linguists indicate that the lower-order process, such as pronunciation and discrimination of sounds, is complete in childhood, while higher-order language functions, like[4] syntactic and semantic aspects, continue to develop until adulthood. Moreover, some studies point out that bilingual children out-perform their monolingual peers in school in terms of problem solving ability and creativity. Finally, bilingual children are more open-minded[5] than monolingual ones toward languages and cultures. Bilingual education develops children's cultural awareness of another group of people. Although some parents are worried about the interference between first and second language learning, the interfering effect is not found in children's language acquisition. Most children are able to learn both languages well. All the above reasons show the benefits of bilingual education for children.

兒童雙語教育

　　我贊成兒童接受雙語教育有幾個理由。首先，兒童比成年人更容易習得純正的發音。兒童時期是學習的關鍵期，在這段期間能習得像母語學習者的口音。此外，研究結果指出雙語兒童能夠區分及發出在他們第一語言不存在的某些聲音，而成人學習者可能缺乏這種能力。一些語言學家指出，較低階的過程如發音和辨音能力，在童年期就發展完成，而高階的語言功能如句法和語意方面，一直到成人期才發展完全。還有，一些研究指出，雙語兒童在學校解決問題的能力和創造力比只學單一語言的同儕能力還要好。最後，雙語兒童在語言和文化上更有開放的態度。雙語教育幫助兒童認識另一群人的文化。雖然有些家長擔心第一和第二語言學習之間的干擾，這干擾現象並沒有在兒童語言學習者上發現。大多數孩子能學好這兩種語言。所有上述原因證明兒童雙語教育的好處。

段落結構 ▶

　　1.主題句（topic sentence）：第一句'I am in favor of bilingual education for children for a number of reasons.'是主題句，點出作者贊成兒童接受雙語教育。

　　2.支持句（supporting sentences）：介於主題句和結論句中間的句子都是支持句，作者提供一些事實及理由來支持論點。

　　3.結論句前的兩個句子用來反駁相反的意見：Although some parents are worried about the interference between first and second language learning, the interfering effect is not found in children's language acquisition. Most children are able to learn both languages well.

　　4.結論句（concluding sentence）：最後一句'All the above reasons show the benefits of bilingual education for children.'是結論句，重述主題句的論點。

字彙與片語 ▶

英　文	詞　性	中　文
in favor of	*prep. phr.*	贊成、支持
bilingual education	*n.*	雙語教育
a number of = several	*prep. phr.*	幾個、一些
acquire	*v.*	習得
authentic pronunciation	*n.*	純正的發音
the critical period	*n.*	關鍵期
native-like	*adj.*	像說母語的
research	*n.*	研究
distinguish	*v.*	區分
exist	*v.*	存在
lack	*v.*	缺乏
indicate	*v.*	指出
discriminate	*v.*	區別
discrimination	*n.*	區別
complete	*adj.*	完全的、完整的
function	*n.*	功能
syntactic	*adj.*	句法的
semantic	*adj.*	語意的
point out	*v.*	指出
out-perform	*v.*	勝過
monolingual	*adj.*	只說一種語言的
peer	*n.*	同儕

英　文	詞　性	中　文
creativity	*n.*	創造力
open-minded	*adj.*	開放的
awareness	*n.*	察覺、認識
are worried about	*v. phr.*	擔心
interference	*n.*	阻礙
benefit	*n.*	好處

文法解釋▶

❶ Children are *more likely* to acquire authentic pronunciation *than* adults.

　　主詞1　　　形容詞比較　　　　　　　　　　　　　　主詞2

本句是一表程度形容詞的比較句，其句子結構如下：

主詞1＋動詞＋形容詞比較＋than＋主詞2

單音節的形容詞字尾加-er成比較級，加-est成最高級。例如：

| tall | taller | tallest |
| high | higher | highest |

如果形容詞是兩個以上的音節所組成的單字，其比較級是在形容詞原級的前面加上more，最高級則加上most。例如：

| beautiful | *more* beautiful | *most* beautiful |
| interesting | *more* interesting | *most* interesting |

❷ The early years of life are the critical period, *in which* an individual can acquire a native-like accent.

which是關係代名詞，在本句中是補述用法，用以補充說明先行詞 'the critical period'，前面有介系詞時，該關係代名詞不能省略。

❸ ~ bilingual children are able to distinguish and pronounce certain sounds which do not exist in their first language, *while* adult learners may lack this ability.

while在本句中是表反義的副詞性連接詞，意思相當於but on the contrary。請看下面範例：

- Some people like coffee, while others hate it.

有些人喜歡喝咖啡，然而有些則討厭咖啡。

❹ ~ the lower-order process, *such* as pronunciation and discrimination of sounds, is complete in childhood, while higher-order language functions, *like* syntactic and semantic aspects, continue to develop until adulthood.

本句中'such as'（例如；像是…），後面只接名詞或名詞詞組，不能接句子。'like'是介系詞後面亦接名詞或名詞詞組。句法上，'such as'和'like'所接的名詞或名詞詞組可視為插入語，補充說明主句要表達的意思。

❺ Bilingual children are more *open-minded* than monolingual ones toward languages and cultures.

本句裡'open-*minded*'是由「形容詞＋擬似分詞」所形成的複合形容詞。這裡的「擬似分詞」是由名詞字尾加上 -ed，句法功用上當形容詞，表示「具有～」的意思。例如：

- a kind-*hearted* man = a man with a kind heart　好心腸的人
- a three-*legged* table = a table with three legs　三條腿的桌子

2. Cosmetic Surgery

I disagree with cosmetic surgery because of the following reasons. First, people who are undergoing the surgery are exposed to the risk of infection or illness. Some celebrities who[1] get rid of excessive amount of fat through the surgery suffer from numbness, ulcer, or even shock. Second, it costs a lot of money to have the operation because it is not medically necessary and usually not covered by health insurance. Third, patients have to endure pain during recovery and those with sensitive skin may need a longer recovery period. Fourth, some people want to get back their original look due to the failure of the surgery. As the saying goes, "Beauty is only skin-deep." We should not judge a person by his or her appearance. Surgeons are not supposed to perform the operation unless[2] the patient is a burn victim who needs skin replacement. While many people think that cosmetic surgery can make[3] them become more physically attractive, it is the vanity that makes them get a better look. I believe that the surgery is for people who suffer from burns or accidents, but[4] not for people who want to improve appearance.

整容手術

我不同意整容手術有以下幾個原因。首先,接受整容手術的人會有感染或生病的風險。一些名人因爲抽脂手術而造成麻木、潰瘍、甚至休克。第二,整容手術花費很高,因爲它不是醫療上必要的手術,通常沒有醫療保險。第三,患者必須忍受恢復過程中的痛苦,而且皮膚敏感的人可能需要較長的恢復期。第四,有些人由於手術失敗想回到原來的樣子。如諺語所説

的「外在美是膚淺的。」我們不應該以貌取人。外科醫生不應該執行整容手術，除非患者是需要更換皮膚的燒傷受害者。雖然很多人認為整容可以使一個人的外表更迷人，這是虛榮心造成的。我相信整容手術是給遭受燒傷或意外事故的人，而不是給想要改善外貌的人。

段落結構 ▶

1.主題句（topic sentence）：第一句'I disagree with cosmetic surgery because of the following reasons.'是主題句，點出作者不同意整容手術。

2.支持句（supporting sentences）：介於主題句和結論句中間的句子都是支持句，作者提供一些事實及理由來支持論點。

3.結論句前一句用來反駁相反的意見：While many people think that cosmetic surgery can make them become more physically attractive, it is the vanity that makes them get a better look.

4.結論句（concluding sentence）：最後一句'I believe that the surgery is for people who suffer from burns or accidents, but not for people who want to enhance appearance.'是結論句，重述主題句的論點。

字彙與片語 ▶

英　文	詞　性	中　文
disagree with	*v. phr.*	不同意
cosmetic surgery	*n.*	整容手術
undergo	*v.*	經歷、接受（手術）
are exposed to	*v. phr.*	暴露於
risk	*n.*	風險

英　文	詞　性	中　文
infection	*n.*	感染
illness	*n.*	生病
celebrity	*n.*	名人（複數celebrities）
get rid of	*v. phr.*	除掉
excessive	*adj.*	多餘的
fat	*n.*	脂肪
suffer from	*v. phr.*	受～之苦
numbness	*n.*	麻木、無感覺
ulcer	*n.*	潰瘍
shock	*n.*	休克
medically	*adv.*	醫療上
necessary	*adj.*	必要地
cover	*v.*	涵蓋
health insurance	*n.*	醫療保險
endure	*v.*	忍受
recovery	*n.*	恢復
sensitive	*adj.*	敏感的
original look	*n.*	原來的樣子
due to = because of	*adv. phr.*	由於、因為
judge	*v.*	判斷
appearance	*n.*	外表
surgeon	*n.*	外科醫師
be supposed to	*v. phr.*	應該
perform	*v.*	進行

英　文	詞　性	中　文
operation	*n.*	手術
unless	*conj.*	除非
patient	*n.*	病人
burn victim	*n.*	燒傷患者
replacement	*n.*	取代、替換
physically attractive	*adv. phr.*	外表有吸引力的
vanity	*n.*	虛榮心

文法解釋 ▶

❶ Some celebrities *who*[1] get rid of excessive amount of *fat* through the surgery suffer from numbness, ulcer, or even shock.

　　本句是關係形容詞子句的句型，關係代名詞who前面沒有逗號，表示限定，修飾先行詞celebrities，用來限定那些做抽脂手術的名人。要注意的是本句中關係形容詞子句who get rid of excessive amount of fat ~…在全句中若去掉，句法雖然沒錯，但語意上會不夠完整。

❷ Surgeons are not supposed to perform the operation *unless* the patient is a burn victim who needs skin replacement.

　　unless（除非、如果不）是表條件的從屬連接詞，語氣上是'if ...not'的加強語氣。請看下面範例：

　　- You will not recover from illness unless you take this medicine.

　　= If you do not take this medicine, you will not recover from illness.

　　你若不服用這藥，你是不會從生病中恢復健康的。

❸ ~ cosmetic surgery can *make* them become more physically attractive, ~…

　　*make*是使役動詞後面接原形動詞。其它有相同句法功能的使役動詞還有*let*、*have*。例如：

　　- I need to have someone take up my luggage.

　　我必須找人提我的行李上來。

　　- My parents never let me go out alone.

　　我父母從不讓我單獨出門。

❹ I believe that <u>the surgery is</u> for people who suffer from burns or accidents, but (the surgery is) not for people who want to improve appearance.

　　*but*是反義連接詞，連接兩個句法功能相同的單字、片語或子句。以本句爲例，but引導的子句與前一子句其主詞、動詞是一樣時，此時'the surgery is' 可以省略。請看下面範例：

　　- He is very clever but lazy.

　　他很聰明，可是很懶惰。

3. The Use of Cell Phone in Public Places

　　I agree with the argument that cell phones should be banned in public places such as libraries, movie theaters, concert hall, and airplane. The most obvious reason is that❶ a phone call interrupts people who are studying in the library or who are watching movies or live performances in the theaters. We are supposed to keep quiet in the library or in a theater, let alone❷ talking on the cell phone. The second reason is that the use of cell phone on the airplane is very dangerous because it will interfere with the communication system. In addition,

the ring of cell phone will distract people who attend worship in the church. Moreover, talking on the phone and completing[3] a transaction at ATM at the same time is impolite because it causes other people to wait longer. Finally, if we have to answer a phone call in public places like in a restaurant or on the train, we need to speak softly. If it is not an emergency, we should tell people that we will call back later. Imagine that someone sitting[4] next to you is talking on the phone for more than ten minutes on the train, how would you feel? For[5] the above reasons, we should turn off the cell phone or switch it to vibration mode in the library, museum, theater, and other public places.

在公共場所使用手機

　　我同意在公共場所如圖書館、電影院、音樂廳和飛機上禁止使用手機。最明顯的原因為講手機會打擾在圖書館看書的人、在電影院看電影的人或在劇院觀賞現場表演的人。在圖書館或在電影院我們應該保持安靜，更不用說講手機。第二個原因是在飛機上使用手機是非常危險的，因為它會干擾通訊系統。此外，手機鈴響會使在教會做禮拜的人不能專心。還有，一邊講電話一邊操作自動提款機是不禮貌的行為，因為它會導致其他人等更久。最後，如果我們需要在公共場所如餐廳或火車上接電話，我們必須輕聲地說話。如果不是緊急情況，我們應該告訴對方稍後再回電。想像在火車上，坐在你旁邊的人講手機超過10分鐘，你的感覺如何？由於上述的原因，我們在圖書館、博物館、劇院和其他公共場所應該關閉手機或把它調為振動模式。

段落結構 ▶

1.主題句（topic sentence）：第一句'I agree with the argument that cell phones should be banned in public places.'是主題句，說明作者立場，不贊成在公共場所使用手機。

2.支持句（supporting sentences）：介於主題句和結論句中間的句子都是支持句，作者提供一些事實及理由來支持論點。

3.結論句（concluding sentence）：最後一句'For the above reasons, we should turn off the cell phone or place it on vibration mode in the library, museum, theater, and other public places.'是結論句，再次強調作者的立場，在公共場所應該關閉手機或把它調為振動模式。

字彙與片語 ▶

英　文	詞　性	中　文
argument	*n.*	論點
cell phone = mobile phone	*n.*	手機
ban = prohibit, forbid	*v.*	禁止
public places	*n.*	公共場所
obvious	*adj.*	明顯的
concert	*n.*	音樂會
interrupt	*v.*	打擾
live performance	*n. phr.*	現場表演
theater	*n.*	電影院、劇院
be supposed to	*v. phr.*	應該
let alone	*v. phr.*	更不用說
interfere	*v.*	干擾

英　文	詞　性	中　文
communication	*n.*	通訊
system	*n.*	系統
distract	*v.*	分散注意力
attend	*v.*	參加
worship	*n.*	敬拜
complete	*v.*	完成
transaction	*n.*	交易
ATM (automated teller machine)	*abbr.*	自動提款機
softly	*adv.*	輕聲地
emergency	*n.*	緊急情況
imagine	*v.*	想像
turn off	*v. phr.*	關閉
switch	*v.*	轉換
vibration	*n.*	振動
mode	*n.*	模式

文法解釋 ▶

❶ *The most obvious reason is that* a phone call interrupts people who are studying in the library ～.

本句的句子結構如下：

... ＋ the ＋形容詞最高級＋單數名詞＋ be ＋ that ＋子句

'The most obvious reason'做主詞，be動詞後面接連接詞that，引導名詞子句。

❷ We are supposed to keep quiet in the library or in a theater, *let alone* talking on the cell phone.

　　let alone是連接詞，表示更不用說、遑論、何況，請再看以下例句：

　　She cannot ride a bicycle, let alone a motorcycle.

　　她不會騎腳踏車，更別說摩托車了。

❸ ~ ⋯, *talking* on the phone and *completing* a transaction at ATM at the same time is impolite ~.　　　　主詞

　　動名詞具有名詞的性質，在句中可當主詞、受詞等。它本身也具有動詞的性質，可以帶受詞或補語。在本句中，動名詞talking後面接補語on the phone，與動名詞completing後面接受詞a transaction和補語at ATM at the same time一起作為整個句子的主詞。

❹ Imagine that someone *sitting* next to you is talking on the phone for more than ten minutes on the train ~.

　　本句是形容詞子句改為「分詞片語」的用法，原句如下：

　　~... someone *who sits* next to you is talking on the phone ~...
　　　先行詞　　關係形容詞子句

　　關係代名詞who與be動詞刪去後就成為分詞片語，修飾前面的不定代名詞someone。

❺ *For* the above reasons, we should turn off the cell phone

　　介系詞for表示原因或理由，相當於because of、on account of（因為、由於）。例如：

　　- He was punished for telling a lie.

　　他因為說謊而受處罰。

4. Lotteries

I am an opponent of the lottery game. The first reason is that a lottery is a type of gambling that players guess which numbers will be drawn by the lottery machine[1]. Players buy lottery tickets in the hope of winning the money. Playing the lottery is regarded as a quick way to get rich. It sounds attractive that one can become a millionaire overnight. However[2], the chance of winning the first prize of a lottery is relatively low. Second, many lottery winners go bankrupt or get into debt because they are not good at managing a large amount of money. They lead an extravagant lifestyle by driving luxury cars, living in mansions, and buying products from luxury brands. Third, some players experience gambling addiction. Even though they know that the odds of winning the jackpot are low, they spend more and more money to chase losses. Fourth, if one won the lottery, he or his family would become the target of kidnapping[3]. One report indicated that a lottery winner was kidnapped and killed because his identity was revealed. Although many supporters of lotteries argue that the lottery fund is used to support public programs such as education and social welfare system, actually only a small portion of the money is spent on public services. I would rather[4] donate the money directly to charity organizations. I believe that the drawbacks of the lottery game outweigh its benefits.

樂透彩券

　　我反對樂透遊戲。第一個原因是它是一種賭博行為，玩家賭注哪個數字會被彩券機抽中。玩家買樂透希望贏錢。買樂透被視為是一個快速致富的途徑。這聽起來很吸引人，人們可以一夕之間成為百萬富翁。然而，贏得頭獎的機會是很低的。第二，許多樂透中獎者破產或陷入債務，因為他們不擅長管理大量的金錢。他們過著奢侈的生活，開豪華車、住豪宅和買名牌貨。第三，一些玩家玩樂透上癮。即使他們知道贏得頭獎的機率很低，他們還是花更多的錢想追回損失的錢。第四，如果一個人中了樂透，他或他的家人將成為綁架的目標。一份報告指出一位樂透中獎者綁架被殺，因為他的身份被揭露出來。雖然許多支持者認為，樂透資金可用在公共建設上，如教育和社會福利制度，實際上只有一小部分的錢用在公共服務上。我寧願直接把錢捐贈給慈善機構。我相信樂透遊戲的缺點大於它的好處。

段落結構 ▶

　　1.主題句（topic sentence）：第一句'I am an opponent of the lottery game.'是主題句，說明作者立場，反對樂透遊戲。

　　2.支持句（supporting sentences）：介於主題句和結論句中間的句子都是支持句，作者提供一些事實及理由來支持論點。

　　3.結論句前一句用來反駁相反的意見：Although many supporters of lotteries argue that the lottery fund is used to support public programs such as education and social welfare system, actually only a small portion of the money is spent on public services.

　　4.結論句（concluding sentence）：最後一句'I believe that the drawbacks of the lottery game outweigh its benefits.'是結論句，再次強調作者的立場，樂透遊戲的缺點大於它的好處。

字彙與片語 ▶

英 文	詞 性	中 文
opponent	*n.*	反對者
lottery	*n.*	樂透
gambling	*n.*	賭博
draw	*v.*	抽出（動詞三態draw, drew, drawn）
in the hope of	*prep. phr.*	希望
is regarded as	*v. phr.*	被視為…
attractive	*adj.*	吸引人的
millionaire	*n.*	百萬富翁
overnight	*adv.*	一夕之間
chance	*n.*	機率
relatively	*adv.*	相當地
bankrupt	*adj.*	破產的
bankruptcy	*n.*	破產
debt	*n.*	債務
a large amount of	*adj. phr.*	大量的
extravagant	*adj.*	奢侈的
luxury	*n.*	豪華
mansion	*n.*	豪宅
luxury brand	*n.*	名牌
addiction	*n.*	上癮
odds	*n.*	機率
jackpot	*n.*	頭獎
chase	*v.*	追回

英　文	詞　性	中　文
target	*n.*	目標
kidnapping	*n.*	綁架
identity	*n.*	身份
reveal	*v.*	揭露
fund	*n.*	資金
social welfare system	*n. phr.*	社會福利制度
donate	*v.*	捐贈
charity organization	*n.*	慈善機構
drawback	*n.*	缺點
outweigh	*v.*	大於、勝過
benefit	*n.*	好處

文法解釋▶

❶ The first reason is <u>that</u> a lottery is a type of gambling *that* players guess *which numbers will be drawn by the lottery machine.*

　　a. 本句中第一個that（字底畫線）引導名詞子句（a lottery ... ~... the lottery machine），作主詞（The first reason）的補語。

　　b. 第二個*that*（斜體字）引導名詞子句（players gusess ... ~... the lottery machine）。

　　c. players guess which numbers will be drawn by the lottery machine，亦即：~... players guess which numbers the lottery machine will draw. 不過，語意上並不是強調誰開出樂透號碼，事實上號碼的開出也不確定是誰操作的，因此這一類句子多用被動語態表示無人稱，如本文

所寫出的句子（players guess which numbers will be drawn by the lottery machine）。此外，本句子亦可用不定詞的結構：~... players guess which numbers to be drawn by the lottery machine.

❷ *However*, the chance of winning the first prize of a lottery is relatively low.

'however'（但是、然而）是表示反義的副詞性連接詞，可放在句首、句中或句尾。請看下面範例：

- I can't oppose your suggestion; however, I won't stand for it.

= I can't oppose your suggestion; I won't stand for it, however.

= I can't oppose your suggestion; I won't, however, stand for it.

我不能反對你的建議，然而我也不會支持。

❸ ~ if one wins the lottery, he or his family will become the target of kidnapping

　　　條件子句　　　　　　　　　主要子句

如果一個人中了樂透，他或他的家人將成為綁架的目標。

主要子句裡：他或他的家人是否成為綁架的目標，要看這個人是否中了樂透為條件。if條件子句中所敘述的是客觀的事實，說話者不知道這個人是否中了樂透，但認為可能性高，因此用直說法。

藉由本句我們順便介紹假設語態的句型。若是與「現在或未來事實相反」的假設，本句動詞的時態如下：

~ if one *won* the lottery, he or his family *would* become the target of kidnapping.

　　條件子句　　　　　　　　　主要子句

　（過去式動詞或助動詞）　　（would, should, might＋原形動詞）

如果一個人中了樂透，他或他的家人將成為綁架的目標。

（事實上，他現在或將來都不會中樂透，他或他的家人也就不會成為綁架的目標。）

若是與「過去事實相反的假設」，本句動詞的時態如下：

~ if one *had won* the lottery, he or his family *would have* become the target ~...

條件子句　　　　　　　　　　主要子句

（had＋動詞過去分詞）　　（would, should, might＋have＋動詞過去分詞）

如果一個人中了樂透，他或他的家人將成為綁架的目標。

（事實上，他都不曾中過樂透，他或他的家人也從未成為綁架的目標）

從上述幾個假設語態的句子，我們發現中文都是用同樣的一句話來表達，說話者與聽話者之間必須互相揣摩所言何意，所指涉的時間是何時。但是在英文的句子裡，動詞的時態變化就清楚地告訴你說話者心裡的想法。此外，有時主要子句裡的動詞時態表示與現在事實相反，條件子句則與過去事實相反。

~ if one *had won* the lottery, he or his family *would* become the target ~...

條件子句　　　　　　　　　　主要子句

（had＋動詞過去分詞）　　（would, should, might＋原形動詞）

如果一個人曾中了樂透，他或他的家人將成為綁架的目標。

（事實上，他之前都不曾中過樂透，他或他的家人現在也不會成為綁架的目標。）

④ I *would rather* donate the money directly to charity organizations.

'would rather'（寧願）是慣用語，後面可再接than表比較，其句子結構如下：

主詞＋would rather＋動詞原形…＋than＋動詞原形…

- I would rather stay at home than go out on a rainy day.

下雨天我寧可待在家，也不要出門。

5. If I were the mayor

If[1] I were the mayor, I would improve the city life from three aspects: providing[2] care for old people[3], increasing employment opportunities, and reducing the crime rate. First, the number of[4] elderly people has rapidly increased in the past decade. I would[5] promote the establishment of elderly community centers which provide a variety of educational and recreational activities for the aged. The elderly need social contact with the outside world to avoid depression or stay away from Alzheimer's disease. Medical care or health care should also be provided for senior citizens to maintain their physiological and psychological well-being. Second, I would increase job opportunities by bringing in new business for unemployed residents or young people who have difficulty finding jobs. Vocational training courses would be provided to improve people's knowledge and job-specific skills that are required in the workplace. Third, crime and unemployment go hand in hand. According to the statistics, poor and unemployed people are more likely to commit crimes. I would reduce the crime rate by offering more job opportunities, taking care of poor people, and implementing severe punishment for criminals. The above three points, I believe, would make the city a better place to live.

如果我是市長

　　如果我是市長，我會從三方面來改善城市生活：照顧老人、增加就業機會以及降低犯罪率。第一，老年人口在過去十年內快速增加。我將推動建立社區老人中心，提供各種教育及娛樂活動，讓老年人有社交機會、與外界接觸，以避免憂鬱症或遠離老人癡呆症（阿茲海默症）。我也會提供老人醫療保健制度，以維持其身心健康。第二，我將增加就業機會，為失業居民或有就業困難的年輕人帶來新工作。也會提供職業培訓課程，增進人們的知識和在職場上所需的特定工作技能。第三，犯罪與失業率息息相關。在統計數據上，窮人與失業者較易於犯罪。我會提供更多就業機會、照顧窮人、和嚴懲犯罪的人，來降低犯罪率。我相信以上三點會讓這城市成為一個適合居住的好地方。

段落結構 ▶

1.主題句（topic sentence）：第一句'If I were the mayor, I would improve the city life from three aspects: providing care for old people, increasing employment opportunities, and reducing the crime rate.'是主題句，說明作者如果擔任市長，會從三方面來改善城市生活。

2.支持句（supporting sentences）：介於主題句和結論句中間的句子都是支持句，作者提供方法如何照顧老人、增加就業機會、以及降低犯罪率。

3.結論句（concluding sentence）：最後一句'The above three points, I believe, would make the city a better place to live.'是結論句，總結以上三點會讓這城市成為一個適合居住的好地方。

字彙與片語 ▶

英 文	詞 性	中 文
mayor	*n.*	市長
employment	*n.*	就業
the crime rate	*n. phr.*	犯罪率
rapidly	*adv.*	快速
decade	*n.*	十年
promote	*n.*	推動
establishment	*n.*	建立
community	*n.*	社區
a variety of	*adj. phr.*	各種
educational	*adj.*	教育的
recreational	*adj.*	娛樂的

英　文	詞　性	中　文
social contact	*n. phr.*	社交
avoid	*v.*	避免
depression	*n.*	沮喪
stay away from	*v. phr.*	遠離
Alzheimer's disease	*n.*	老人癡呆症（阿茲海默症）
medical care	*n. phr.*	醫療照顧
health care	*n.*	保健
maintain	*v.*	維持
physiological	*adj.*	身體的
psychological	*adj.*	心理的
well-being	*n.*	健康
unemployed	*adj.*	失業的
resident	*n.*	居民
vocational training	*n. phr.*	職業培訓
job-specific skills	*n. phr.*	特定工作技能
require	*v.*	需要
workplace	*n.*	職場
go hand in hand	*v. phr.*	息息相關
commit crimes	*v. phr.*	犯罪
implement	*v.*	執行
severe	*adj.*	嚴厲的
punishment	*n.*	懲罰
criminal	*n.*	罪犯

文法解釋 ▶

❶ If I were the mayor, I would improve the city life from three aspects: ~…

   條件子句   主要子句

（過去式動詞或助動詞）   （would, should, might＋原形動詞）

如果我是市長，我會從三方面來改善城市生活。

（事實上，我現在或將來都不會是市長，我也沒法從三方面來改善城市生活。）

❷ ~ card for old people, ~

本文中 old people、the elderly、elderly people、the aged、senior citizens 都是指老年人。寫作時，可用不同的詞彙表達相同意思的字，避免一直使用同樣的字。

❸ ~ *providing* care for old people, *increasing* employment opportunities, and *reducing* the crime rate.

在本句中，動名詞 providing 後面接受詞 care 和補語 for old people，動名詞 increasing 後面接受詞 employment opportunities，動名詞 reducing 後面接受詞 the crime rate。

❹ The number of elderly people has rapidly increased in the past decade.

本句中，「the number of＋複數名詞＋單數動詞」，但是「a number of＋複數名詞＋複數動詞」。試比較下列範例：

- The number of students in the class is 30.

這班學生數目是三十人。

- A number of students in the class are from Taipei. (a number of = several)
班上有些學生來自台北。

❺ First, ~… I *would* promote the establishment of elderly community centers

　　本文中，列舉三點想要做的事情，句子裡皆用助動詞would是因為省略了條件子句if I were the mayor；表示與現在或未來事實相反的假設。

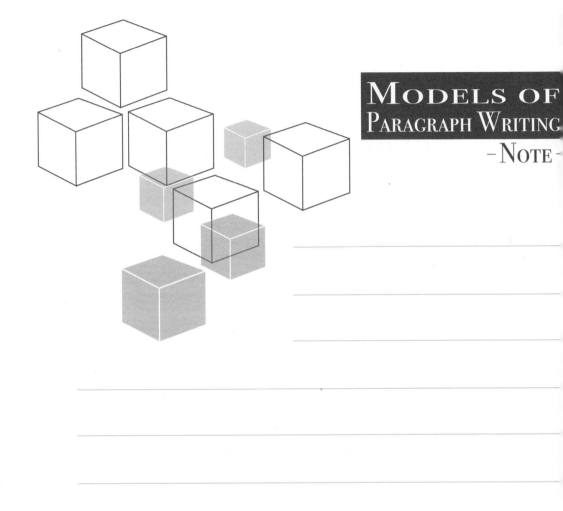

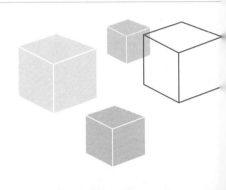

分類型段落
CLASSIFICATION PARAGRAPHS

　　分類型段落把事物做分類，根據分類的原則（organizing principle），對每一類別做介紹與解釋。例如：嗜好可以根據狀態分爲靜態嗜好（sedentary hobbies）和動態嗜好（dynamic hobbies），也可以根據場所分爲室內活動（indoor hobbies）和戶外活動（outdoor hobbies）。分類時，每一類別不能重複。比如說把嗜好分爲dynamic hobbies和outdoor hobbies，這樣的分類就重複了，動態嗜好也可能是室外活動。分類型段落主題句常用的句型爲：

1. (Something) can be divided/grouped/classified/categorized into several types/groups.

2. We can divide/group/classify/categorize (something) into several types/groups.

以下是分類型段落我們提供的五篇範文：

第一篇文章 Types of hobbies 描述嗜好的種類

第二篇文章 Types of music 描述音樂的種類

第三篇文章 Friends I have had 描述我遇過朋友的種類

第四篇文章 Restaurants in the city 描述城市裡餐廳的種類

第五篇文章 Popular TV programs 描述受歡迎電視節目的種類

1. Types of Hobbies

Hobbies can be grouped into two main types: indoor hobbies and outdoor hobbies. Indoor hobbies include reading books, playing musical instruments, collecting special items, and so on. Some people enjoy reading novels or short stories while[1] others like to read comic books or manga. Reading enables people to broaden knowledge, increase imagination, and develop creativity. In addition, playing a musical instrument brings joy to people around us. One can play the piano or the violin to entertain oneself, family, and friends. Moreover, collecting special items such as[2] stamps and coins is also a good hobby because it enlarges our understanding of the world and serves as a legacy for future family generation. On the other hand, outdoor hobbies contain photography, cycling, hiking, sports activities, and so forth. Photography is an enjoyable hobby that one spends time capturing beautiful moments and exploring different places. Furthermore, both cycling and hiking are healthy hobbies. People can go cycling[3] in the countryside to enjoy the fresh air or go hiking in the hills to get close to the nature and relieve stress. Sports like basketball, baseball, football, and soccer, are competitive leisure activities enjoyed by many young people. Whatever it may be[4], a hobby is an activity that gives one joy and pleasure.

嗜好的種類

　　嗜好主要分為兩種類型：室內的活動和戶外的活動。室內的活動包括閱讀書籍、演奏樂器、收集特殊物品等等。有些人喜歡看小說或短篇故事，而有些人喜歡看漫畫。閱讀使人們增長知識、增進想像力、和培養創造力。此外，演奏樂器能帶給我們周圍的人歡樂。彈奏鋼琴或拉小提琴的人可以娛樂自己、家人和朋友。還有，收集特殊物品如郵票和硬幣也是一個很好的嗜好，因為它增進了我們對世界的認識，並成為留給後代的遺產。另一方面，戶外活動包含攝影、騎單車、爬山、球類運動等等。攝影是個令人喜愛的嗜好，讓人捕捉美麗的時刻和探索不同的地方。此外，騎單車和爬山都是健康的活動。人們可以在鄉間騎單車，享受清新的空氣，或是去爬山，親近大自然和紓解壓力。球類運動如籃球、棒球、美式足球和英式足球，是很多年輕人休閒時喜歡做的有競爭力的運動。不管它是什麼嗜好，都是帶給人歡樂的活動。

段落結構 ▶

1.主題句（topic sentence）：第一句'Hobbies can be grouped into two main types: indoor hobbies and outdoor hobbies.'是主題句，說明嗜好可分為室內和戶外的活動。

2.支持句（supporting sentences）：介於主題句和結論句中間的句子都是支持句，分別說明室內和戶外活動包含哪些。

3.結論句（concluding sentence）：最後一句'Whatever it may be, a hobby is an activity that gives one joy and pleasure.'是結論句。

字彙與片語 ▶

英　文	詞　性	中　文
hobby	*n.*	嗜好
be grouped into	*v. phr.*	分類、分組
indoor	*adj.*	室內的
outdoor	*adj.*	室外的
musical instrument	*n.*	樂器
comic book	*n.*	漫畫（書）
manga	*n.*	連環漫畫書
enable	*v.*	使能夠
broaden	*v.*	增長
imagination	*n.*	想像力
creativity	*n.*	創造力
piano	*n.*	鋼琴
violin	*n.*	小提琴

英　文	詞　性	中　文
entertain	*v.*	娛樂
stamp	*n.*	郵票
coin	*n.*	硬幣
enlarge	*v.*	擴展
serve as	*v. phr.*	當作是
legacy	*n.*	遺產
generation	*n.*	世代、一代
photography	*n.*	攝影
cycling	*n.*	騎單車
hiking	*n.*	健行
capture	*v.*	捕捉
explore	*v.*	探索
countryside	*n.*	鄉間
get close to	*v. phr.*	親近
nature	*n.*	大自然
relieve	*v.*	紓解
stress	*n.*	壓力
football	*n.*	美式足球、橄欖球
soccer	*n.*	英式足球
competitive	*adj.*	競爭力的

文法解釋 ▶

❶ Some people enjoy reading novels or short stories *while* others like to read comic books or manga.

'while'是表示反義的「副詞連接詞」，這樣稱呼它是因為句法上，它具有副詞的功用，但是意義上卻與連接詞相同，也就是說它不能用來連接單字或片語，只能用來連接子句或句子。

本範文中另外有表示累積的副詞連接詞：in addition（此外）、moreover（此外）、furthurmore（此外）。句法上都是引導一個子句來加強對前一句的說明。請看下面範例：

- Your project is excellent; in addition, it can save a lot of money.

你的計畫太好了，而且它可以省下很多錢。

- He is a good man. Moreover, he is honest and reliable. Furthermore, no one can replace him as an executive of the plan.

他是個好人，而且誠實又可靠，更重要的是，作為這項計畫的執行長，沒有人能夠取代他的位置。

此外，besides與except的差別：

· besides（除……之外、還有……）。例如：

- Besides John, Jane went swimming.

除了約翰，珍也去游泳。（約翰和珍都去游泳）

· except（除……之外）。例如：

- We went swimming except John.

我們去游泳了，除了約翰以外。（約翰沒有去游泳）

❷ ~ collecting special items such as stamps and coins is also a good hobby…

　　本句中'such as'（例如；像是……），後面只接名詞或名詞詞組，不能接句子。另一句：Sports like basketball, baseball, football, and soccer, are competitive leisure activities ~ …其中'like'是介系詞後面可接名詞或名詞詞組。句法上，'such as'和'like'所接的名詞或名詞詞組可視為插入語，補充說明主句要表達的意思。

❸ People can go cycling in the countryside to enjoy the fresh air or go hiking in the hills to get close to the nature and relieve stress.

　　有關動詞{go / play / do}＋運動的用法，我們說明如下：

- Go ＋ 戶外運動（v-ing）。例如：go cycling, go hiking, go fishing, go jogging, go skiing, go swimming, go bowling, go roller-skating, go surfing

- Play ＋ 球類。例如：play basketball, play baseball, play football, play soccer, play badminton, play golf, play tennis, play table tennis, play volleyball

- Do ＋ 運動。例如：do aerobics, do gymnastics, do yoga

❹ *Whatever* it may be, a hobby is an activity that gives one joy and pleasure.

　　whatever有兩個用法，第一是它引導名詞子句，在句中可當主詞或受詞，請看以下例句：

Whatever he said was not true.（whatever he said是主詞）

You can take away what ever you want.（whatever you want是受詞）

第二是引導副詞子句，可用no matter what替換。本文中的句子可改寫成如下：

· *Whatever* it may be, a hobby is an activity that gives one joy and pleasure.
  = No matter what

2. Types of Music

Music is classified into several types on the basis of genre, including classical music, pop music, country music, rock music, jazz, and others. First, classical music is the art music produced in the western world from the medieval period to the present time. It presents an aesthetic, elegant, and graceful style. It is often played in the form of sonata, concerto, and symphony with string, woodwind, brass, and percussion instruments. The most[1] important characteristic is that it never loses its appeal over time. Second, pop music aims to appeal to a general audience. The songs reflect existing trends. Unlike classical music, it does not last a long time but varies frequently according to fashion. Third, country music originates in the western and southern United States. It has a simple melody, a memorable story line, and a chorus, which[2] make it easier for people to recall and sing the song. Fourth, rock music has a strong rhythm and is usually played with electric guitars and drums. Its powerful sound brings energy and vitality to the audience. Fifth, jazz is a style of music developed by African Americans in the southern United States. It is characterized by improvisation, in which[3] the players create the music without preparation. No matter what kind of music it is, music is believed to enrich people's life.

音樂的種類

　　音樂根據其風格分為幾種類型，包括古典音樂、流行音樂、鄉村音樂、搖滾樂、爵士樂、還有其他種類。首先，古典音樂是西方世界從中世紀時期至今創作出的藝術音樂。它呈現出唯美、優雅、和典雅的風格。它經常以奏鳴曲、協奏曲和交響樂的演奏形式出現，演奏樂器有弦樂、木管、銅管和打擊樂器。最重要的特點是，隨著時間的過去，它從來沒有失去它的吸引力。第二，流行音樂主要吸引一般觀眾，歌曲反映了現有的潮流趨勢。與古典音樂不同的是，它不會持續很長一段時間，而是根據流行趨勢變化頻繁。第三，鄉村音樂起源於美國西部和南部。它有簡單的旋律、讓人印象深刻的故事情節和重複歌詞的副歌，這使得人們容易回憶起這類的歌。第四，搖滾樂有著強烈的節奏，演奏的樂器通常是電吉他和鼓。其強有力的聲音帶給觀眾活力和生氣。第五，爵士樂是非裔美國人在美國南部發展出來的音樂風格。它的特點是即興創作，演奏者不用事前準備而創造出音樂。不管它是什麼樣的音樂，音樂豐富了人們的生活。

段落結構 ▶

1.主題句（topic sentence）：第一句‘Music is classified into several types on the basis of genre, including classical music, pop music, country music, rock music, jazz, and others.’是主題句，說明音樂根據其風格分爲古典音樂、流行音樂、鄉村音樂、搖滾樂、爵士樂。

2.支持句（supporting sentences）：介於主題句和結論句中間的句子都是支持句，分別說明每種音樂的風格和特色。

3.結論句（concluding sentence）：最後一句‘No matter what kind of music it is, music is believed to enrich people's life.’是結論句。

字彙與片語 ▶

英　文	詞　性	中　文
be classified into	v. phr.	分爲
on the basis of	prep. phr.	根據
genre	n.	風格
classical music	n. phr.	古典音樂
pop music	n.	流行音樂
country music	n.	鄉村音樂
rock music	n.	搖滾樂
jazz	n.	爵士樂
produce	v.	創作
medieval	adj.	中世紀的
present	adj.	目前的
aesthetic	adj.	唯美的

英　文	詞　性	中　文
elegant	*adj.*	優雅的
graceful	*adj.*	典雅的
sonata	*n.*	奏鳴曲
concerto	*n.*	協奏曲
symphony	*n.*	交響樂
string	*n.*	弦
woodwind	*n.*	木管
brass	*n.*	銅管
percussion	*n.*	打擊
appeal	*n.*	吸引
appeal to	*v.*	吸引
audience	*n.*	觀眾
reflect	*v.*	反映
existing trends	*n. phr.*	現有的潮流趨勢
last	*v.*	持續
vary	*v.*	變化
frequently	*adv.*	頻繁地
according to	*prep. phr.*	根據
fashion	*n.*	流行
originate	*v.*	起源於
melody	*n.*	旋律
memorable	*adj.*	難忘的
story line	*n.*	故事情節
chorus	*n.*	合唱

英　文	詞　性	中　文
recall	*v.*	回憶
rhythm	*n.*	節奏
energy	*n.*	活力
vitality	*n.*	活力、生氣
is characterized by	*v. phr.*	以……爲特點
improvisation	*n.*	即興創作
preparation	*n.*	準備
enrich	*v.*	豐富

文法解釋▶

❶ The *most* important characteristic is that it never loses its appeal over time.

　　本範文中用最高級形容詞表達最好、最優的結構如下：

　　「... ＋ the ＋ 形容詞最高級 ＋ 單數名詞 ＋ be ＋ that ＋ 子句」

　　'The most important characteristic' 作主詞，be動詞後面接連接詞that引導的子句it never loses its appeal over time當主詞補語。

❷ It has a simple melody, a memorable story line, and a chorus, *which* make it easier for people to recall and sing the song.

　　關係代名詞which前面有逗號，表示非限定，替代「非人」的動物或無生物。which在本句中替前面子句裡提到的幾個項目：a simple melody、a memorable story line and a chorus，做動詞make的主詞。'make'在本句中授與動詞，後面接直接受詞it（指的是country music）與受詞補語（easier for people ~...）。

❸ It is characterized by improvisation, *in which* the players create the music without preparation.

關係代名詞which在本句中是補述用法，用以補充說明先行詞 'improvisation'，前面有介系詞時，該關係代名詞不能省略。事實上介系詞in 亦不可省略，'in which' 有強調此一場景或在此情況下的意思。

3. Friends I Have Had

I classified my friends into three groups: best friends I have known for a long time❶, good friends who❷ share similar interests with me, and ordinary friends. I have a few best friends, who care about me and stay with me in both good and bad times. We share happiness and sorrow with each other. As the saying goes, "A friend in need is a friend indeed." They walked through the difficult times of my life. They are also the friends whom❸ I can trust in and share my secrets with. The second group of my friends are those who are interested in music. We talk about favorite songs, singers, composers, and bands. Sharing a favorite interest with good friends gives us motivation, inspiration, enthusiasm in our life. The third group, ordinary friends, is no more than❹ acquaintances who greet each other with a smile or a nod. Some of them are also called fair-weather friends, who are friends in pleasant time but are not in time of trouble. What is worse, some friends only show up when they need a favor. They leave after getting what they want. Among these friends, only those who are genuine and honest will be friends forever.

我遇過的朋友

　　我把我的朋友歸為三類：我已經認識很長一段時間的最好的朋友、與我志趣相投的好朋友和普通朋友。我有幾個最好的朋友，他們關心我，不管是快樂或困難的時候都和我在一起。我們分享彼此的快樂和悲傷。如諺語所說的，患難見真情。他們陪我走過生命中的困難時期。他們是我可以信任和分享秘密的朋友。第二類朋友是對音樂有興趣的朋友。我們談論喜歡的歌曲、歌手、作曲家和樂團。與好朋友分享最喜愛的興趣，給予我們生活中的動機、靈感和熱忱。第三類是普通朋友，只在遇到時會微笑或點頭的朋友。他們其中有一些也被稱為可以共享樂、不能共患難的朋友。更糟的是，有些朋友只在需要幫忙的時候才出現。當他們得到想要的東西後就離開了。在這些朋友中，只有那些真誠和誠實的朋友才是永遠的朋友。

段落結構 ▶

　　1.主題句（topic sentence）：第一句'I classified my friends into three groups: best friends I have known for a long time, good friends who share similar interests with me, and ordinary friends.'是主題句，作者把朋友歸為三類：已經認識很長一段時間的最好的朋友、志趣相投的好朋友和普通朋友。

　　2.支持句（supporting sentences）：介於主題句和結論句中間的句子都是支持句，分別說明每一類朋友的特色。

　　3.結論句（concluding sentence）：最後一句'Among these friends, only those who are genuine and honest will be friends forever.'是結論句，強調只有真誠和誠實的朋友才是永遠的朋友。

字彙與片語 ▶

英　文	詞　性	中　文
classify	*v.*	分類
best friends	*n.*	最好的朋友
good friends	*n.*	好朋友
ordinary friends	*n.*	普通朋友
happiness	*n.*	快樂
sorrow	*n.*	悲傷
walk through	*v. phr.*	走過、經歷
trust	*v.*	信任
secret	*n.*	秘密
composer	*n.*	作曲家
band	*n.*	樂團
motivation	*n.*	動機
inspiration	*n.*	靈感
enthusiasm	*n.*	熱忱
acquaintance	*n.*	相識的人
greet	*v.*	問候、招呼
nod	*n.*	點頭
fair-weather friends	*n.*	可以共享樂、不能共患難的朋友
pleasant time	*n. phr.*	歡樂時光
in time of trouble	*prep. phr.*	需要幫忙的時候
what is worse	*conj.*	更糟的是
show up	*v.*	出現
favor	*n.*	幫忙

英　文	詞　性	中　文
genuine	*adj.*	眞正的
forever	*adv.*	永遠的
A friend in need is a friend indeed.	*proverb.*	患難見眞情

文法解釋▶

❶ ...~ best friends I have known for a long time,~···

本範文中用最高級形容詞的結構如下：

'... + the +最高級+名詞+ that + ... +（ever）+ ...'

- He is the best pianist that I have ever seen.

他是我見過最好的鋼琴家。

❷ - ~ good friends <u>*who* share similar interests with me</u>, ~...

關係形容詞子句表限定

- I have a few best friends, <u>*who* care about me and stay with me</u> ~...

關係形容詞子句表非限定

　　第一句關係代名詞who引導的關係形容詞子句是限定用法，句法上前面沒有逗號，語意上表示那些志趣相同的好朋友。第二句who前面有逗號，引導的關係形容詞子句是非限定用法，或稱作補述用法，用來補充說明那幾個最要好朋友的特點。

❸ They are also the friends *whom* I can trust in and share my secrets with.

'whom'是受格關係代名詞作及物動詞或介系詞的受詞。在本句中作介系詞in和with的受詞。介系詞亦可放在whom前面：

請再看下面範例：

- He has few friends *whom* he can talk *with*.

= He has few friends *with whom* he can talk.

他沒有很多朋友可以聊天。

❹ Ordinary friends are *no more than* acquaintances who greet each other with a smiler or a nod.

以下我們整理no more than與no less than用法的片語：

‧no more than = only（只）

- I have no more than twenty dollars.

我只有二十塊錢。

‧not less than = as mush as

- He has no less than ten million dollars.

他有多達一千萬的存款。

‧no more ~ than = not ~ any nore than（和⋯一樣不⋯）

- He is no more reliable than Ana.

他和安娜一樣不可靠。

‧not less ~ than = as ⋯ as

- He is no less rich than John.

他和約翰一樣富有。

4. Restaurants in the City

The restaurants in the city can be divided into three types: gourmet restaurants, casual dining restaurants, and fast food restaurants. Gourmet restaurant offers the finest food, high-quality service, and an elegant atmosphere. Customers dress nicely to dine in gourmet restaurants. The chefs use specialized cooking techniques to prepare gourmet dishes. The waiters are trained professionally to serve diners. The second type, casual dining restaurants, serves food at a moderate price. This kind of restaurant usually provides table service that the waiter takes orders and brings the dishes. There is one type of casual dining restaurants, called family style restaurants, where❶ food is served on large plates with family or friends sitting around the table. The third type is the fast food restaurants, which is characterized by the speed of service and convenience. The service style is counter service that one or more cashiers greet and take orders from customers, take payments, and issue receipts. Fast food restaurants usually offer drive through service that allows customers to buy food without leaving their cars. MacDonald's and Kentucky are examples of fast food chains. Among the three types of restaurants, casual dining restaurants and fast food restaurants attract a wider customer base because the foods are more affordable.

城市餐廳的種類

　　城市裡的餐廳可分為三種類型：美食餐廳、休閒餐廳、速食店。美食餐廳提供最好的菜、高品質的服務以及優雅的氣氛。顧客穿著漂亮到美食餐廳用餐。廚師用專門的烹飪技術準備美味佳餚。服務生有受過專業的訓練。第二類是休閒餐廳，供應價格適中的菜。通常這一類餐廳提供餐桌服務，服務生點菜把菜餚帶上桌。有一種休閒餐廳叫做家庭式餐廳，大家圍成一桌共享桌上菜餚。第三類是速食店，特色是快速和便利，採用櫃檯服務，一個或多個收銀員幫客人點餐、收錢、給發票。速食店通常提供得來速服務，讓客人不用下車也能買餐。麥當勞和肯德基是兩個速食連鎖店的例子。這三類餐廳中，休閒餐廳和速食店吸引較多的客人，因為消費者較負擔得起。

段落結構 ▶

1.主題句（topic sentence）：第一句'The restaurants in the city can be divided into three types: gourmet restaurants, casual dining restaurants, and fast food restaurants.'是主題句，作者把餐廳分為三類：美食餐廳、休閒餐廳、速食店。

2.支持句（supporting sentences）：介於主題句和結論句中間的句子都是支持句，分別說明每種餐廳的特色。

3.結論句（concluding sentence）：最後一句'Among the three types of restaurants, casual dining restaurants and fast food restaurants attract a wider customer base because the foods are more affordable.'是結論句。

字彙與片語 ▶

英　文	詞　性	中　文
gourmet	*n.*	美食
casual dining restaurant	*n.*	休閒餐廳
fast food	*n. phr.*	速食
high-quality	*adj.*	高品質的
elegant	*adj.*	優雅的
atmosphere	*n.*	氣氛
dress	*v.*	穿著
dine	*v.*	用餐
chef	*n.*	廚師
specialized	*adj.*	專門的
technique	*n.*	技術
professionally	*adv.*	專業地

英　文	詞　性	中　文
diner	*n.*	用餐的人
moderate	*adj.*	適中的
table service	*n. phr.*	餐桌服務
take orders	*v. phr.*	點菜
is characterized by	*v. phr.*	以～爲特色
speed	*n.*	快速
convenience	*n.*	便利
counter service	*n. phr.*	櫃檯服務
cashier	*n.*	收銀員
payment	*n.*	付款
receipt	*n.*	發票
drive through service	*n. phr.*	得來速服務
chain	*n.*	連鎖店
affordable	*adj.*	負擔得起

文法解釋 ▶

❶ There is ～, called family style restaurants, *where* food is served on
　　large plates, ～ .
　　　　　　　　　　　　　　　　　先行詞　　　　　　　形容詞子句

　　關係副詞是兼有連接詞作用的副詞，以本句爲例，where用於表示地方
的名詞之後，引導形容詞子句。

　　關係副詞和關係代名詞的主要功能都是引導形容詞子句，不過關係副
詞句法上是作副詞用，關係代名詞則是具有代名詞的功用。試比較下面的句
子：

- This is the city *where* I was born. （正）

- This is the city which I was born. （誤）

〔本句關係代名詞which加上in，句法功用上等於關係副詞where: *This is the city in which I was born.*〕

- This is the city where I visited yesterday. （誤）

〔where不具有代名詞的功用，不能當形容詞子句裡動詞visited的受詞〕

- This is the city *which* I visited yesterday. （正）

❷ 我們藉由本篇範文的句子（除了'S＋V'和'S＋V＋IO＋DO'之外），複習英文的五大句型。

・S＋V（主詞＋完全不及物動詞）

- The train stopped.
        S   V

動詞stop之後不須要接何字詞即可表達完整句意，這類動詞稱爲「完全不及物動詞」。

・S＋V＋SC（主詞＋不完全不及物動詞＋主詞補語）

- MacDonald's and Kentucky are examples of fast food chains.
        S   V   SC

動詞are之後必須要接適當的字詞，像是名詞或形容詞才能表達完整的句意，這類動詞稱爲「不完全不及物動詞」。本句中examples of fast food chains是用來補充說明主詞的字稱爲「主詞補語」。

・S＋V＋O（主詞＋完全及物動詞＋受詞）

- Gourmet restaurant offers the finest food,~ and an elegant atmosphere.
        S   V   O

動詞offers之後必須接名詞或名詞詞組，做句法上的受詞，才能表達完整的句意，這類動詞稱爲「完全及物動詞」。

・S＋V＋O＋OC（主詞＋不完全及物動詞＋受詞＋受詞補語）

- This kind of restaurant usually provides table service that the waiter takes
　　　S　　　　　　　V　　　　O　　　形容詞子句作OC

orders and brings the dishes.
　　　　　　OC

動詞provides之後除了接名詞或代名詞之外，必須再接另一個字詞或形容詞子句，補充説明句法上當受詞的名詞table service，這樣的句意才完整，這類動詞稱爲「不完全及物動詞」。

・S＋V＋IO＋DO（主詞＋授與動詞＋間接受詞＋直接受詞）
・S＋V＋DO＋介＋IO

- I bought him some books. = I bought some books for him.
　S　V　IO　DO　　　S　V　　　DO　　介　IO

及物動詞bought又稱爲授與動詞，之後必須接兩個受詞，一是表示人的直接受詞him，另一個是表示物的間接受詞some books。

5. Popular TV Programs

Popular TV programs in Taiwan include the following types: education, news, food, music, travel, shopping, sports, variety shows, talk shows, and soap opera. First, educational programs such as Discovery and National Geographic channels introduce various phenomena in science, nature, history, culture, and increase our knowledge of the world. Second, through the news channels, people

keep up with what is happening locally and globally. Third, music channels provide information about popular music and singers for their fans. Fourth, food channels introduce delicacies, local snacks, and special restaurants around Taiwan. Fifth, travel programs include tours of tourist attractions and resorts, and visits to significant cities in Taiwan and around the world. Sixth, through the shopping channels or phone-in TV shows, people can buy items or bid for them. Seventh, sports channels broadcast sports news and games. Eighth, variety shows consist of songs, dances, and comedy skits. Ninth, a talk show invites a lot of famous people to talk about their experiences. Tenth, a soap opera is a fictional drama based on the daily lives of multiple characters. Among the ten popular TV programs, eight of them are recreation and entertainment shows.

受歡迎的電視節目

　　台灣受歡迎的電視節目包括以下幾種類型：教育、新聞、美食、音樂、旅遊、購物、體育、綜藝節目、談話節目、連續劇。首先，教育節目如Discovery與國家地理頻道介紹各種在科學、自然、歷史、文化的現象，並增加我們對世界的認識。第二，新聞頻道讓人們知道地方及全球發生的事情。第三，音樂頻道提供流行音樂和歌手的資訊給歌迷。第四，美食頻道介紹台灣各地的美味佳餚、地方小吃、以及特色餐廳。第五，旅遊節目包括參觀旅遊景點和度假勝地，以及參觀台灣和世界各地的重要城市。第六，購物頻道中，人們可以出價購買物品。第七，體育頻道播出體育新聞和競賽。第八，綜藝節目包括歌曲、舞蹈、搞笑短劇。第九，談話節目邀請很多著名人士談論他們的經驗。第十，連續劇是以日常生活為題材，虛構而成的故事情節。在這十種受歡迎的電視節目，其中八個是休閒和娛樂節目。

段落結構▶

　　1.主題句（topic sentence）：第一句'Popular TV programs in Taiwan include the following types: education, news, food, music, travel, shopping, sports, variety shows, talk shows, and soap opera.'是主題句，列出台灣受歡迎的電視節目有教育、新聞、美食、音樂、旅遊、購物、體育、綜藝節目、談話節目、連續劇。

　　2.支持句（supporting sentences）：介於主題句和結論句中間的句子都是支持句，分別介紹每種電視節目。

　　3.結論句（concluding sentence）：最後一句'Among the ten popular TV programs, eight of them are recreation and entertainment shows.'是結論句，總結受歡迎的電視節目中，其中八個是休閒和娛樂節目。

字彙與片語 ▶

英 文	詞 性	中 文
program	*n.*	節目
channel	*n.*	頻道
phenomenon	*n.*	現象（複數形 phenomena）
science	*n.*	科學
nature	*n.*	自然
history	*n.*	歷史
culture	*n.*	文化
keep up with	*v. phr.*	跟上
locally	*adv.*	地方上的
globally	*adv.*	全球的
fan	*n.*	歌迷、粉絲
delicacy	*n.*	美味佳餚
snack	*n.*	小吃
tour	*n.*	旅遊
tourist attraction	*n.*	旅遊景點
resort	*n.*	度假勝地
visit	*n.*	參觀
significant	*adj.*	重要的
bid	*v.*	出價
broadcast	*v.*	播出
variety show	*n*	綜藝節目
consist of	*v.*	包括
comedy skits	*n*	搞笑短劇

英　文	詞　性	中　文
talk show	*n.*	談話節目
soap opera	*n.*	連續劇
recreation	*n.*	休閒
entertainment	*n.*	娛樂

文法解釋 ▶

❶ 數詞分為基數詞與序數詞。數詞表舉例如下：

數字	基數	序數	簡寫
1	one	first	1st
2	two	second	2nd
3	three	third	3rd
4	four	fourth	4th
5	five	fifth	5th
6	six	sixth	6th
7	seven	seventh	7th
8	eight	eighth	8th
9	nine	ninth	9th
10	ten	tenth	10th
11	eleven	eleventh	11th
12	twelve	twelfth	12th
13	thirteen	thirteenth	13th
14	fourteen	fourteenth	14th

數字	基數	序數	簡寫
15	fifteen	fifteenth	15th
16	sixteen	sixteenth	16th
17	seventeen	seventeenth	17th
18	eighteen	eighteenth	18th
19	nineteen	nineteenth	19th
20	twenty	twentieth	20th
21	twenty-one	twenty-first	21st
22	twenty-two	twenty-second	22nd
23	twenty-three	twenty-third	23rd
24	twenty-four	twenty-fourth	24th
30	thirty	thirtieth	30th
40	forty	fortieth	40th
50	fifty	fiftieth	50th
60	sixty	sixtieth	60th
70	seventy	seventieth	70th
80	eighty	eightieth	80th
90	ninety	nintieth	90th
100	hundred	one hundredth	100th

❷ 藉由本篇範文，我們介紹幾個介系詞的用法。

in:

- 表示「位置、在……地方」。

  - Popular TV programs *in* Taiwan include the following types: ~.

- 表示「關於、在……方面」。

  - Geographic channels introduce various phenomena *in* science, nature, ~.

of:

- 用在「名詞＋of＋名詞」的結構中，後面的「of＋名詞」表示所有格。
  - ... ~ increase our knowledge *of* the world.
  - ... ~ travel programs include tours *of* tourist attractions and resorts, and visits to significant cities in Taiwan and around the world.
- 用於表示「組成」的動詞片語中。
  - Eighth, variety shows *consist of* songs, dances, and comedy skits.
- 用於表示「部份、份量」，of 銜接前後部份關係。
  - Tenth, a talk show invites *a lot of* famous people to talk about their experiences.
  - Among the ten popular TV programs, eight *of* them are recreation and entertainment shows.

through:

- 表示「媒介、方法」，作「藉、經由」解。
  - Second, *through* the news channels, people keep up with what is ~.
  - Sixth, *through* the shopping channels or phone-in TV shows, people can buy items or bid for them.

about:

- 表示「關於、有關」。
  - ... ~ music channels provide information *about* popular music and singers for their fans.
  - Tenth, a talk show invites a lot of famous people to talk *about* their experiences.

around:

- 表示「環繞、在……四周」，通常指的是靜態的位置。

    - ... ~ travel programs include tours of tourist attractions and resorts, and visits to significant cities in Taiwan and *around* the world.

with:

- 表示「跟上」。

    - ... ~ people keep up with what is happening locally and globally.

to:

- 表示「目的」。

    - ... ~ travel programs include tours of tourist attractions and resorts, and visits to significant cities in Taiwan and around the world.

for:

- 表示「爲了」。

    - ... ~ music channels provide information about popular music and singers *for* their fans.

    - ... ~ people can buy items or bid *for* them.

among:

- 表示「在……之中」，用在多數且相同的事物中，後面接複數的名詞。

    - *Among* the ten popular TV programs, eight of them are recreation and entertainment shows.

過程段落
PROCESS PARAGRAPHS

　　過程段落描述如何完成一件事情，詳細說明並明確解釋每個步驟。描述過程段落時需要注意以下幾點：

1. 選擇你熟悉的主題，清楚明確的描述每個步驟。

2. 每個步驟按照時間的順序先後列出來，用連接詞如first, second, next, before, after, finally等連接。

3. 任何步驟、細節、或是需要特別注意的過程都要寫出來。

4. 通常文章裡會有祈使句（imperative sentences）和代名詞（you）的使用。

以下是過程段落我們提供的五篇範文：

第一篇文章 Writing a good paragraph 描述如何寫好一個英文段落

第二篇文章 Reading an English newspaper 描述如何閱讀英文報紙

第三篇文章 Applying for a job 描述如何求職

第四篇文章 A marriage proposal 描述如何求婚

第五篇文章 Making a pizza 描述如何做披薩

1. Writing a Good Paragraph

Writing a good paragraph is not difficult if you follow the guidelines. First, you brainstorm[1] about the topic and write down all the ideas that[2] come into your mind. You cross out some ideas and generate new ideas. After you gather many ideas, you decide which ones will be included in the paragraph and start[3] organizing them. Then, begin to work on the first draft. Your paragraph should have a topic sentence, several supporting sentences, and a concluding sentence. When you write the topic sentence, make sure that it states the main idea of the paragraph. Then, write several supporting sentences that give information to support and explain the topic. Next, write a concluding sentence to bring the paragraph to a logical conclusion. You can either[4] restate the main idea of the paragraph or offer a suggestion to end a paragraph. After you finish the first draft, correct and improve the content of the text. Check if all the sentences are related to the topic. Remove any irrelevant sentences. Finally, proofread the paragraph and check for mistakes. By[5] following these guidelines, you can write a good paragraph.

如何寫好一個英文段落

要寫好一個段落並不難，如果你遵循以下原則。首先，先對題目做腦力激盪，寫下跟此題目你所有的想法。刪掉一些想法，並加入新的想法。當你收集很多想法後，你決定哪些要寫進這篇文章，然後開始組織這些想法。接著開始寫初稿。你的段落應要有一個主題句、數個支持句和一個結論句。當你寫主題句時，注意要寫出該段的主題。然後寫幾個支持句來支持和解釋主

題句。接下來結論句為整段做一個合邏輯的總結。你可以重述該段的主題或提供建議來結束這個段落。在你完成初稿後，要改正和改善文本內容。檢查是否所有句子都與主題相關。刪除任何無關的句子。最後，校對並檢查整個段落。遵循這些原則，你可以寫出一個好的段落。

段落結構▶

1.主題句（topic sentence）：第一句'Writing a good paragraph is not difficult if you follow the guidelines.'是主題句，指出要寫好一個段落並不難。

2.支持句（supporting sentences）：介於主題句和結論句中間的句子都是支持句，分別介紹如何寫好一個段落的步驟。

3.結論句（concluding sentence）：最後一句'By following these guidelines, you can write a good paragraph.'是結論句，重述主題句，只要遵循這些原則就能寫出一個好段落。

字彙與片語▶

英 文	詞 性	中 文
paragraph	*n.*	段落
guideline	*n.*	方針、準則
brainstorm	*v.*	腦力激盪
cross out	*v. phr.*	刪掉
generate	*v.*	產生
gather	*v.*	收集
include	*v.*	包括
organize	*v.*	組織

英　文	詞　性	中　文
draft	*n.*	初稿
topic sentence	*n. phr.*	主題句
supporting sentences	*n. phr.*	支持句
concluding sentence	*n. phr.*	結論句
make sure	*v. phr.*	確定
state	*v.*	陳述
main idea	*n. phr.*	主題
logical	*adj.*	合邏輯的
restate	*v.*	重述
related	*adj.*	相關的
irrelevant	*adj.*	無關的
proofread	*v.*	校對

文法解釋▶

❶ 祈使句在句法上主詞通常省略不說，動詞用原形。以下我們列舉本範文
　的例句：

- You *brainstorm* about the topic and *write down* all the ideas that come int
  your mind.

- You *cross out* some ideas and *generate* new ideas.

- After you finish the first draft, *correct* and *improve* the content of the text.

❷ First, you brainstorm about the topic and write down all the ideas *that* come into your mind.

關係代名詞that只能用於表限定的關係形容詞子句，前面沒有逗號。that 具有代名詞的功用，句法上亦可由which替代，表示「非人」的動物或無生物。

❸ ~ and *start organizing* them.

動詞start後面接動名詞或不定詞，意義上是一樣的。同樣的動詞還有 begin（開始）、continue（繼續）等等。請看範例：

- He began to play the piano.
= He began playing the piano.
他開始彈鋼琴。

不過，有些動詞像是remember（記得）、forget（忘記）、regret（後悔）、stop（停止）等等接動名詞或不定詞為受詞，意義上是不一樣的。請看範例：

- He stopped to play the piano.
他停下來，（然後）開始彈鋼琴。
≠ He stopped playing the piano.
他停止彈鋼琴。

❹ You can *either* restate the main idea of the paragraph *or* offer a suggestion to end a paragraph.

「either...or（不是……就是）」是選擇性連接詞，用來連接對等的單字、片語或子句。如果連接兩個主詞時，動詞必須和第二個主詞一致。請看範例：

- Either he or you are to blame.
不是他就是你該受責備。

127

❺ By following these guidelines, you can write a good paragraph.

介系詞「by＋動名詞」表示方式和方法，請再看下面範例：

- Here people earn their living by selling handicrafts.

這兒人們靠出售手工藝品來謀生。

2. Reading an English Newspaper

Learning to read an English newspaper is important because it will help you improve reading skills. First, you need to know about the various sections of a newspaper. Briefly look over each section, read the headlines, and choose the articles that interest❶ you. After you find an article that you want to read, read the first or two paragraphs which will provide important information about the event. Read no more than two paragraphs unless❷ the article is of great interest to you. When you read, scan the text instead of reading word by word. You can get the gist of the article by picking up some key words. Do not worry about the new words. Keep❸ reading and try to guess the meanings of unknown words from the context or look up important words in the dictionary after reading. Remember that it❹ is unnecessary to understand every word of the article. If you constantly read newspapers everyday, you may encounter the same words several times and remember them easily. Gradually you will increase English vocabulary. If you follow the instruction, you will be able to read an English newspaper.

閱讀英文報紙

　　學習閱讀英文報紙是重要的，因為它會幫助你增進閱讀技巧。首先，你需要知道報紙包含不同版面。快速看一下每個部分，閱讀標題，並選擇你感興趣的文章。當你找到想讀的文章後，閱讀第一段或前兩個段落有關該事件的重要報導。每篇文章閱讀不要超過兩段，除非文章是你很感興趣的。當你閱讀時，掃描內文而不是一個字一個字的讀。你可以從一些關鍵字了解整篇文章的大意。不要擔心新的單字。繼續閱讀，試著從上下文猜單字的意思，或閱讀後再查重要的單字。記住，閱讀時不需要知道每一個字的意思。如果你持續每天閱讀報紙，你可能會遇到同樣的單字好幾次，這樣很容易把它們記起來。漸漸地，你會增加英語字彙量。如果你採用這個方法，你將能夠閱讀英文報紙。

段落結構 ▶

1.主題句（topic sentence）：第一句'Learning to read an English newspaper is important because it will help you improve reading skills.'是主題句，指出學習閱讀英文報紙是重要的。

2.支持句（supporting sentences）：介於主題句和結論句中間的句子都是支持句，說明如何閱讀英文報紙。

3.結論句（concluding sentence）：最後一句'If you follow the instruction, you will be able to read an English newspaper.'是結論句，呼應主題句，採用這個方法，你將能夠閱讀英文報紙。

字彙與片語 ▶

英　　文	詞　　性	中　　文
various	*adj.*	不同的
section	*n.*	版面
briefly	*adv.*	快速地
look over	*v. phr.*	看一下
headline	*n.*	標題
event	*n.*	事件
no more than	*adv. phr.*	只有、不超過
unless	*conj.*	除非
scan	*v.*	掃描
instead of	*prep. phr.*	代替
gist	*n.*	要點、主旨
pick up	*v. phr.*	挑出

英　文	詞　性	中　文
key words	*n.*	關鍵字
worry about	*v. phr.*	擔心
unknown words	*n.*	不認識的字
context	*n.*	上下文
look up	*v. phr.*	查詢
unnecessary	*adj.*	不需要的
constantly	*adv.*	持續地
encounter	*v.*	遇到
gradually	*adv.*	漸漸地
increase	*v.*	增加
vocabulary	*n.*	字彙
instruction	*n.*	指示

文法解釋 ▶

❶ ~ and choose the articles that *interest* you.

　　本句中及物動詞interest可以用下面其它的表達的句型：

　　- ~ and choose the articles that *you are interested in.*

　　- ~ and choose the articles that *are interesting to you.*

　　關係代名詞that只能用於表示限定的關係形容詞子句，而且前面不可以接介系詞。that可以用which替代，這個情況下介系詞可放在which前面。請看下面範例：

　　- ~ and choose the articles *in which you are interested.*

　　= ~ and choose the articles *which you are interested in.*

131

❷ Read no more than two paragraphs *unless* the article is of great interest to you.

    unless（除非、如果不）是表條件的從屬連接詞，語氣上是'if ...not'的加強語氣。請看下面範例：

    - You will fail unless you study harder from now on.

    = If you do not study harder from now on, you will fail.

    從現在開始你若不更用功點，你會被當掉。

❸ *Keep* reading and try to guess the meanings of unknown words ~.

    動詞'keep'後面只能接動名詞做受詞，不可以接不定詞to，表達動作持續進行的意思。同樣動詞只能接動名詞做受詞的還有mind（介意）、finish（完成）、quit（停止）、enjoy（喜歡）、admit（承認）、suggest（建議）等等。請看下面範例：

    - I enjoy playing tennis with him.

    我很喜歡和他打網球。

    - He admitted tellig a lie.

    他承認說謊。

❹ Remember that *it is unnecessary to* understand every word of the article.

    *It*是虛主詞或形式上的主詞，代替本句後面所要說的不定詞'to understand every word of the article'。換句話說，不定詞片語才是真正的主詞。不定詞意義上的主詞是泛指一般人或事物時，意義上的主詞可省略。若要將意義上的主詞表明，可加上'for you'，請看下面例句：

    - It is unnecessary *for you* to understand every word of the article.

3. Applying for a Job

Applying for a job involves several steps. The first step is to find the suitable position. Read the position description thoroughly about specific skills and experiences the employer is seeking. The next step is writing a resume. In your resume, make sure you have clear headings. List your work experiences and education in reverse chronological order. Highlight your qualifications that meet the needs of the employer. Include other relevant information such as special skills that make you stand out as the right person for the job. After the company receives your resume and offers you an interview, research the company and gather as much information as possible[2] through the Internet, magazines, or current employees. This will help you prepare both[3] to answer interview questions and to ask the interviewer questions. Then, proper interview etiquette is important. Remember[4] to greet your interviewer with a friendly smile and a firm handshake. During the interview, maintain good eye contact, pay attention, and look interested. Finally, send a thank-you letter to the interviewer after the interview. Your job application procedure is complete if you follow all these steps.

如何求職

　　求職包含幾個步驟。第一是找合適的職位。詳讀應徵職務說明，了解雇主尋求的特定技能和經驗。下一步是寫履歷。寫履歷時，確認你有明確的標題。列出你的學經歷，順序從時間最近的寫到過去。強調你的資格符合雇主的需求。包含其他相關資料如特殊技能，這能突顯你為這項工作的合適人

選。當公司收到你的履歷並提供你面試機會時，盡可能從網路、雜誌、或現有員工，收集有關這公司的資料。這將幫助你準備回答面試的問題和詢問面試人員問題。接下來，適當的面試禮儀是重要的。記住看到面試人員時，要面帶微笑，握手要堅定有力。面試過程中，保持良好的目光接觸、專心和表現對此工作有興趣。面試結束後，寫封感謝信給面試人員。如果你遵循這些步驟，你的求職程序就完成了。

段落結構 ▶

1. 主題句（topic sentence）：第一句 'Applying for a job involves several steps.' 是主題句，指出求職包含幾個步驟。

2. 支持句（supporting sentences）：介於主題句和結論句中間的句子都是支持句，說明如何求職的步驟。

3. 結論句（concluding sentence）：最後一句 'Your job application procedure is complete if you follow all these steps.' 是結論句，呼應主題句，遵循這些步驟，完成求職程序。

字彙與片語 ▶

英　文	詞　性	中　文
apply for a job	*v. phr.*	求職
involve	*v.*	牽涉、包含
suitable	*adj.*	合適的
position description	*n. phr.*	職務說明
thoroughly	*adv.*	詳細地
specific	*adj.*	特定的

英　文	詞　性	中　文
employer	*n.*	雇主
seek	*v.*	尋求
resume	*n.*	履歷
make sure	*v. phr.*	確認
heading	*n.*	標題
reverse	*adj.*	相反的、顛倒的
chronological	*adj.*	依時間前後順序排列記載的
highlight	*v.*	強調
qualification	*n.*	資格
meet the needs	*v. phr.*	符合需求
relevant	*adj.*	相關的
stand out	*v. phr.*	突顯
research	*v.*	調查、研究
current	*adj.*	現有的
employee	*n.*	員工
proper	*adj.*	適當的
etiquette	*n.*	禮儀
firm handshake	*n. phr.*	握手堅定有力
maintain	*v.*	保持
eye contact	*n. phr.*	目光接觸
pay attention	*v. phr.*	專心
look interested	*v. phr.*	表現對～有興趣
application procedure	*n. phr.*	求職程序
complete	*adj.*	完成的

文法解釋 ▶

❶ 動名詞具有名詞的性質，在句中可當主詞、受詞等。它本身也具有動詞的性質，可以帶受詞或補語。以下我們先列出在本篇範文中使用動名詞的句子：

- <u>Applying for a job</u> involves several steps.
 主詞

- The next step is <u>writing a resume</u>.
 補語

第一句動名詞applying後面接介系詞補語for a job作整句的主詞，第二句動名詞writing後面接受詞a resume作be動詞補語。

❷ ~ gather *as much information as possible*

本句亦可寫成'gather *as much information as you can , ~*'

❸ ~ prepare *both* <u>to answer interview questions</u> *and* <u>to ask the interviewer questions</u>.　　不定詞片語　　　　　　　　　不定詞片語

'both ... and ...'是累積式連接詞，連接兩個語法上相同的單位，像是名詞、代名詞、形容詞、不定詞等等。

❹ *Remember* to greet your interviewer with a friendly smile and a firm handshake.

動詞remember後面可接不定詞或動名詞，但意義上不一樣。本句是祈使句，remember後面接不定詞，表示該動作greet（招呼、迎接）尚未去做，有提醒記得去完成的意思。

若是接動名詞表示該動作已完成，曾經有過的經驗。例如：

- I remember telling him to come to the party tonight.
我記得告訴過他，要來今晚的派對。

136

4. A Marriage Proposal

You can make proposing to your girlfriend a memorable moment by carefully planning for this event. Before you propose[1], both of you should agree to spend the rest of life with each other. Next, consider[2] asking her parents for approval to show respect for her family. Then you can proceed to propose marriage to your future wife. You arrange an appropriate time and place to propose to her. You can choose a special day such as the anniversary of your first date or a particular time of her favorite season. Take your girlfriend to the place where you first met or treat her a surprise dinner at her favorite restaurant. Make sure your girlfriend feels comfortable with the way you propose. If she likes to have[3] her family and friends witness the event, you can prepare a party for her. If she prefers a private moment with you, find a place for only two of you. Show her the ring, tell her why you want to marry her, and what[4] marriage means for you. Finally, give her a kiss or a hug if she says yes. You will have a beautiful and unforgettable marriage proposal if you plan every detail well.

求婚

經由仔細策劃，你的求婚會是難忘的回憶。求婚之前，你們兩人應要同意與對方攜手共度一生。接下來，考慮徵求她父母的同意，以表示對她家人的尊重。然後你就可以進行求婚的動作。你安排適當的時間和地點向她求婚。你可以選擇一個特別的日子，比如你們第一次約會的紀念日，或是選擇她最喜歡的季節的一個特定時間。帶你的女友去你們第一次見面的地方或是請她去最喜歡的餐廳，給她一個驚喜晚餐。確認你的求婚方式讓你女友覺得

自在。如果她喜歡有家人和朋友見證求婚，你可以為她舉辦一場派對。如果她較喜歡與你獨處，找一個只有你們兩個人的地方。拿出戒指告訴她，你為什麼要和她結婚，婚姻對你的意義是什麼。如果她答應了，給她一個吻或擁抱。如果計劃好每個細節，你將有個美麗而難忘的求婚回憶。

段落結構▶

1.主題句（topic sentence）：第一句'You can make proposing to your girlfriend a memorable moment by carefully planning for this event.'是主題句，指出如果仔細策劃，求婚會是難忘的回憶。

2.支持句（supporting sentences）：介於主題句和結論句中間的句子都是支持句，說明如何求婚。

3.結論句（concluding sentence）：最後一句'You will have a beautiful and unforgettable marriage proposal if you plan every detail well.'是結論句，呼應主題句，如果計畫好每個細節，將有個美麗而難忘的求婚回憶。

字彙與片語▶

英　文	詞　性	中　文
propose	*v.*	求婚
marriage proposal	*n.*	求婚
memorable	*adj.*	難忘的
moment	*n.*	片刻
event	*n.*	事件
consider	*v.*	考慮
approval	*n.*	同意

英　文	詞　性	中　文
respect	*n.*	尊重
proceed	*v.*	進行
arrange	*v.*	安排
appropriate	*adj.*	適當的
anniversary	*n.*	週年紀念日
date	*n.*	約會
particular	*adj.*	特別的
treat	*v.*	請客
make sure	*v. phr.*	確認
comfortable	*adj.*	自在的
witness	*v.*	見證
prefer	*v.*	較喜歡
ring	*n.*	戒指
hug	*n.*	擁抱
unforgettable	*adj.*	難忘的
detail	*n.*	細節

文法解釋 ▶

❶ Before you propose, both of you should agree to spend the rest of life with each other.

本句中propose為不及物動詞，後面省略掉to her。

❷ Next, *consider* asking her parents for approval to show respect for her family.

　　動詞consider後面只能接動名詞為受詞，不可接不定詞。同樣的動詞或片語還有：avoid（避免）、burst out（突然）、enjoy（喜歡）、mind（介意）、admit（承認）、finish（完成）、suggest（建議）、can't help（不得不）等等。

❸ If she likes to *have* her family and friends witness the event, ~.

　　本句中動詞have作使役動詞用，其句子結構為：〔have＋人＋原形動詞〕。動詞have亦可用get替代，但是後面要用介系詞to：〔get＋人＋to＋原形動詞〕。本句若改用have動詞，句子寫成如下：

　　- If she likes to get her family and friends to witness the event, ~.

❹ ~, tell her why you want to marry her, and *what* marriage means for you.

　　why you want to marry her為間接問句，原本的句子為Why do you want to marry her?同樣的，what marriage means for you，原本的句子為What does marriage mean for you?。句法上同樣的句型如下：

　　- What time is it now?
　　現在幾點鐘了？
　　- I don't know what time it is now.
　　我不知道現在幾點。

5. Making a Pizza

Making a pizza is not complicated when you follow the step-by-step[1] recipe. First, you can get a ready-made crust in the supermarket to save time in preparing dough. Place the crust on a baking tray and spread a coat of olive oil over the top of the crust. Next, spread spaghetti sauce or homemade pizza sauce across[2] the crust. Toppings are added over the sauce, depending on whatever you like. Pre-cook raw meat toppings, such as chicken or beef. Vegetables like onions or peppers can also be pre-cooked to release water. Do not pile on a lot of toppings, or[3] the crust will not be crispy. Put the heavier meat toppings on the bottom layer and the lighter vegetable toppings on the top layer. Finally, sprinkle mozzarella cheese over the toppings. After preheating the oven to 425F degrees[4], you put the pizza in the oven for approximately 20 minutes until the crust is golden-brown and the cheese is melted. Remove the pizza from the oven and let[5] it cool for a few minutes. Slice the pizza into pieces and you are ready to enjoy the pizza. You will be able to make a pizza at home easily by following the instruction.

如何做披薩

按照食譜一步一步做披薩的過程並不複雜。首先,你可以到超市買現成的餅皮,以節省準備麵團的時間。把餅皮放在烤盤上並在餅皮上塗上一層橄欖油。接下來,在餅皮上抹上義大利麵醬或是自製的披薩醬。然後加上任何你喜歡的材料。生肉如雞肉或牛肉要先煮一下。洋蔥或青椒等蔬菜也可以

先預煮釋出水分。不要堆放很多材料,否則餅皮不會酥脆。把較重的肉類放底層而較輕的蔬菜放上層。最後,撒上mozzarella起司。烤箱預熱到華氏425度後,把披薩放進烤箱烤約20分鐘,直到呈現金黃色和起司融化即可出爐。披薩從烤箱取出後先放涼。把披薩切塊,你就可以享受披薩了。按照這些步驟,你將能夠輕鬆在家做披薩。

段落結構 ▶

1.主題句(topic sentence):第一句'Making a pizza is not complicated when you follow the step-by-step recipe.'是主題句,指出做披薩的過程並不複雜。

2.支持句(supporting sentences):介於主題句和結論句中間的句子都是支持句,說明如何做披薩的步驟。

3.結論句(concluding sentence):最後一句'You will be able to make a pizza at home easily by following the instruction.'是結論句,呼應主題句,按照這些步驟就能輕鬆在家做披薩。

字彙與片語 ▶

英　文	詞　性	中　文
complicated	*adj.*	複雜的
recipe	*n.*	食譜
ready-made crust	*n. phr.*	現成的餅皮
dough	*n.*	麵團
baking tray	*n. phr.*	烤盤(烘焙的盤子)
spread	*v.*	塗上(原意是擴展)

英　文	詞　性	中　文
coat	*n.*	層
olive oil	*n. phr.*	橄欖油
spaghetti sauce	*n. phr.*	義大利麵醬
homemade	*adj.*	自製的
topping	*n.*	添加物
depend on	*v. phr.*	視……而定
raw	*adj.*	生的、未煮過的
onion	*n.*	洋蔥
pepper	*n.*	青椒
release	*v.*	釋出
pile on	*v. phr.*	堆上
crispy	*adj.*	酥脆的
bottom layer	*n. phr.*	底層
top layer	*n. phr.*	上層
sprinkle	*v.*	撒上
cheese	*n.*	起司
preheat	*v.*	預熱
oven	*n.*	烤箱
approximately	*adv.*	大約
melt	*v.*	融化
remove	*v.*	取出
slice	*v.*	切片
instruction	*n.*	指示

文法解釋▶

❶ Making a pizza is not complicated when you follow the *step-by-step* recipe.

step by step為一形容詞片語修飾名詞recipe. step by step亦可用來修飾動詞，請看下面範例：

- If you want to play the piano well, you should learn it step by step.

如果你想要彈好鋼琴，你應該循序漸進去學。

❷ Next, spread spaghetti sauce or homemade pizza sauce *across* the crust.

介系詞across作橫過解釋，意思是將義大利醬塗抹在整面脆皮上。

❸ Do not pile on a lot of toppings, *or* the crust will not be crispy.

or是選擇性連接詞，在此作「否則」解釋。請再看下面例句：

- Hurry up, or we will not catch the train.

= If you do not hurry up, we will not catch the train.

快一點，否則我們趕不上火車。

❹ After preheating the oven to *425F degrees*, ~…

在美國是使用華氏溫度（Fahrenheit degree），不同於其他世界大多數國家，包括台灣，使用攝氏溫度（Celsius degree）。我們也順便認識一下這兩種測量溫度的換算公式：

➡ 攝氏溫度×9/5＋32＝華氏溫度

➡ （華氏溫度－32）× 5/9＝攝氏溫度

舉例來説：

➡ 攝氏218.3℃×9/5＋32 = 425 ℉（華氏）

➡（華氏425℉ – 32）× 5/9 = 218.3℃（攝氏）

❺ Remove the pizza from the oven and *let* it cool for a few minutes.

　　let用來表示命令的祈使句通常用於第一或第三人稱其句型爲：〔let＋受詞＋原形動詞〕。請再看下面範例：

- Let me see what happened.

讓我看看怎麼回事。

- Let him come in.

讓他進來。

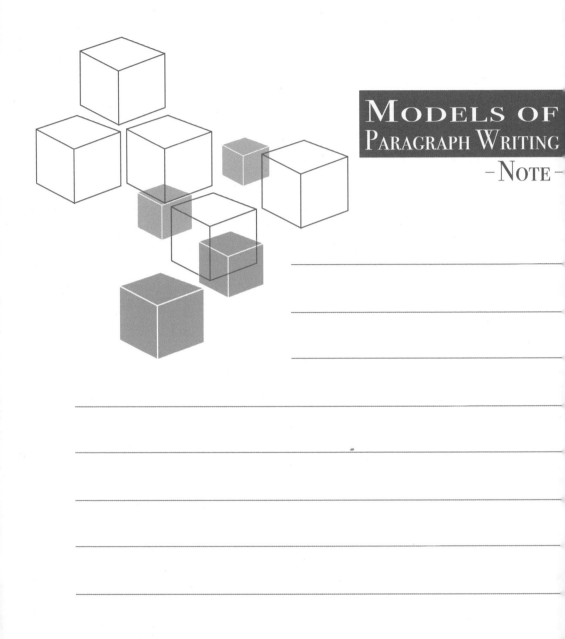

MODELS OF
PARAGRAPH WRITING
-NOTE-

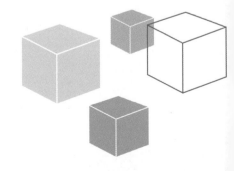

比較與對比的段落
COMPARISON & CONTRAST PARAGRAPHS

比較與對比的段落比較兩樣事物的相同點（similarities）和不同點（differences）。此類型的文章結構有兩種：

1.Block method：先列出前者的特點，再列出後者的特點。

2.Point-by-point method：分別就每項特點比較兩者的差異。

例如要比較大學生活和高中生活，有兩種寫法：(1) 先列出大學生活的特色，再列出高中生活的特色。(2) 分別就課業、活動、自由度等各方面來比較大學生活和高中生活的差異。

在比較與對比的段落裡，表示兩者相同的用語有：be similar to, the same as, alike, identical, have…in common。表示兩者不同的用語有：be different from, unlike, while, however, on the other hand, in contrast, on the contrary。

以下是比較與對比的段落我們提供的五篇範文：

第一篇文章 College life and high school life 比較大學生活與高中生活

第二篇文章 Homeschooling and regular schooling 比較在家教育和學校教育

第三篇文章 Wedding customs in Taiwan and in the USA 比較台灣和美國的婚禮習俗

第四篇文章 Chinese food and Japanese food 比較中國菜和日本菜

第五篇文章 Tablets and laptops 比較平板電腦和筆記型電腦

1. College Life and High School Life

College life **is different from** high school life in several aspects. One major difference is the academic subjects. High school students have to study all subjects **while**[1] college students specialize in certain subjects. In college, students can choose the elective courses they are interested in[2] besides the required courses. The second difference is that college life brings more freedom. High school students follow the pre-arranged class schedule; **however**, college students arrange their own schedule. College students have more responsibilities and freedom to manage time, such as balancing schoolwork and leisure activities. The third difference is the social life. **Unlike** most high school students who live at home, college students live in the dormitory. They learn to live with new friends, communicate with roommates, and adjust living habits. Fourth, under[3] the pressure of preparing for the college entrance exam, high school students may not participate in extracurricular activities. **On the other hand**, college students usually join clubs. They learn about leadership, social skills, and how to make decisions. In short, college life and high school life vary in terms of academic subjects, freedom, social life, and extra-curricular activities.

大學生活與高中生活

　　大學生活與高中生活在幾個方面是不一樣的。一個主要的不同點是學科。高中生必須學習所有科目，而大學生主修某專門學科。在大學裡，除了必修課，學生可以選擇他們感興趣的選修課。第二個不同點是大學生活帶來較多的自由。高中生按照預先安排的課程上課，但是，大學生安排自己的課程表。大學生有更多的責任和自由管理時間，例如在課業和休閒活動間取得平衡。第三個不同點是社交生活。不像大多數高中生住在家裡，大學生住宿舍。他們學習與新朋友生活、與室友溝通和調適生活習慣。第四，由於準備大學入學考的壓力，高中生可能不會參加課外活動。但另一方面，大學生通常參加社團。他們學習領導能力、社交技巧以及如何做決定。總之，大學生活在學科、自由度、社交生活和課外活動這幾方面與高中生活是不同的。

段落結構 ▶

1.主題句（topic sentence）：第一句'College life is different from high school life in several aspects.'是主題句，指出大學生活與高中生活在幾個方面是不一樣的。

2.支持句（supporting sentences）：介於主題句和結論句中間的句子都是支持句，本文採用point-by-point method分別就各個方面比較大學生活與高中生活的差異。

3.結論句（concluding sentence）：最後一句'In short, college life and high school life vary in terms of academic subjects, freedom, social life, and extra-curricular activities.'是結論句，重述主題句，大學生活在學科、自由度、社交生活和課外活動這幾方面與高中生活是不同的。

4.粗體字爲表示兩者不同的用語：be different from, unlike, while, however, on the other hand。

字彙與片語 ▶

英　文	詞　性	中　文
is different from	*v. phr.*	與～不同
aspect	*n.*	方面
major	*adj.*	主要的
academic subjects	*n. phr.*	學科
specialize in	*v. phr.*	主修
elective courses	*n. phr.*	選修課
required courses	*n. phr.*	必修課
freedom	*n.*	自由

英　文	詞　性	中　文
schedule	*n.*	時間表、課程表
arrange	*v.*	安排
manage time	*v. phr.*	管理時間
balance	*v.*	平衡
leisure activities	*n. phr.*	休閒活動
social life	*n. phr.*	社交生活
dormitory	*n.*	宿舍
adjust	*v.*	調適
living habits	*n. phr.*	生活習慣
pressure	*n.*	壓力
entrance exam	*n. phr.*	入學考
participate in	*v.*	參加
extracurricular activities	*n. phr.*	課外活動
club	*n.*	社團
leadership	*n.*	領導能力
make decisions	*v. phr.*	做決定
vary	*v.*	不同
in terms of	*prep. phr.*	就～而論、在～方面

文法解釋▶

❶ High school students have to study all subjects *while* college students specialize in certain subjects.

　　'while'在本句中是「然而」的意思，表示反義的「副詞連接詞」，這樣

151

稱呼它是因為句法上，它具有副詞的功用，但是意義上卻與連接詞相同，也就是說它不能用來連接單字或片語，只能用來連接子句或句子。有關副詞連接詞的用法讀者可參考 V.（過程段落）的範文1。

❷ In college, students can choose the elective courses they _are interested in_ besides the required courses.

　　本句中，'they are interested in'是一關係形容詞子句，前面省略了關係代名詞that或which。若使用關係代名詞that，只能用於表示限定的關係形容詞子句，而且前面不可以接介系詞。此外，that可以用which替代，這個情況下介系詞可放在which前面。請看下面範例：

- ~ the elective courses _that_ they are interested _in_.

= ~ the elective courses _which_ they are interested _in_.

= ~ the elective courses _in which_ they are interested.

- *~ the elective courses in that they are interested.（符號*表示本句是錯的）

❸ Fourth, _under_ the pressure of preparing for the college entrance exam, high school students may not participate in extracurricular activities.

　　本句是用介系詞片語來組合句子，原本兩個句子：

High school students are under the pressure of preparing for college entrance exam.

High school students may not participate in extracurricular actirities.

合併而成。

2. Homeschooling and Regular Schooling

Homeschooling and regular schooling are **different** in several ways. The first difference is the learning environment. In home education, children are taught by parents or tutors at home, **while** in school education, students are taught by qualified teachers in formal settings of public or private schools. The second difference is the curriculum. In homeschooling, parents have the flexibility to choose the materials that better meet children's individual needs. Since[1] all children have different development levels and learn at different paces, parents can provide materials at the right level of their children and set their own schedule. **In contrast**, the curriculum and schedule of school education are determined by schools. Teachers may not be able to pay attention to each student's strengths and weaknesses or attend to each student's special needs. The third difference is that homeschooled children lack social interaction with classmates that the school counterparts[2] have. School students have the opportunity to make friends and interact with other children. Finally, homeschooled children experience less[3] competition and peer pressure than school students. By considering the above differences of homeschooling and regular schooling, parents can decide the better education for their children.

在家教育和學校教育

在家教育和學校教育在幾個方面是不同的。第一個是不同的學習環境。在家教育指的是由家長或家庭教師來教育小孩,而學校教育是在正式的教育場合如公立或私立學校由合格教師來教學。第二個是不同的課程。在家教育的家長可以有彈性的選擇較能滿足兒童個別需求的教材。由於所有的孩子都有不同的發展,學習速度也不一樣,家長可以提供適合小孩程度的教材和設定自己的時間表。相反的,學校教育的課程和時間表由學校決定。教師可能無法注意每個學生的強項和弱點,照顧每個學生的特殊需求。第三個不同的地方是,在家教育的孩子缺乏學校的學生才有的社交互動。學校的學生有機會交朋友和與其他孩子互動。最後,在家教育的孩子比學校的學生有較少的競爭力和同儕壓力。考慮上述在家教育和學校教育的差異,家長可以為孩子選擇最好的教育。

段落結構 ▶

1.主題句（topic sentence）：第一句'Homeschooling and regular schooling are different in several ways.'是主題句,指出在家教育和學校教育兩者在幾個方面是不同的。

2.支持句（supporting sentences）：介於主題句和結論句中間的句子都是支持句,本文採用point-by-point method分別就各個方面比較在家教育和學校教育的差異。

3.結論句（concluding sentence）：最後一句'By considering the above differences of homeschooling and regular schooling, parents can decide the better education for their children.'是結論句,建議家長比較在家教育和學校教育的差異,選擇一個較適合小孩的教育方式。

4.粗體字為表示兩者不同的用語：be different, while, in contrast。

字彙與片語 ▶

英　文	詞　性	中　文
homeschooling	*n.*	在家教育
regular schooling	*n. phr.*	學校教育
tutor	*n.*	家庭教師
while	*conj.*	然而、可是
qualified	*adj.*	合格的
formal	*adj.*	正式的
public	*adj.*	公立
private	*adj.*	私立
curriculum	*n.*	課程
flexibility	*n.*	彈性
material	*n.*	教材
meet the needs	*v. phr.*	滿足需求
pace	*n.*	速度
schedule	*n.*	時間表
in contrast	*prep. phr.*	相反的
determine	*v.*	決定
pay attention to	*v. phr.*	注意
strength	*n.*	長處
weakness	*n.*	弱點
attend to	*v. phr.*	注意、照顧
social interaction	*n. phr.*	社交互動
counterpart	*n.*	對應的人或物
competition	*n.*	競爭力

英　文	詞　性	中　文
peer pressure	*n. phr.*	同儕壓力
consider	*v.*	考慮

文法解釋 ▶

❶ *Since* all children have different development levels and learn at different paces, parents can provide ~.

從屬連接詞since表示原因，常用在句首，等於because。

❷ ~ homeschooled children lack social interaction with classmates that the school *counterparts* have.

counterparts：對應的人或物，這裡指的是homeschooled children對應的人，也就是school students.

❸ Finally, homeschooled children experience *less* competition and peer pressure *than* school students.

本句是不及或差等比較，其句子結構是〔... less + 名詞 + than...〕或〔... less + 原級adj. / adv. + than ...〕。例如：

- She is less busy than I (am).

她沒有我忙。

以下我們整理less幾個相似用法的片語：

・no less than = as {much / many} as（多達）

- I have no less than 60 students in this class.

這班我有六十多個學生。

‧ not less than = at least（最少）

- I stayed in Madrid not less than twenty days.

我在馬德里至少停了二十天。

‧ no less ~ than = as ~ as（和……一樣……）

- He is no less reliable than Ana.

= He is as reliable as Ana.

他和安娜一樣可靠。

‧ not less ~ than = perhaps + 比較級 + than ~（也許比……更……）

- He is not less intelligent than Mary.

= He is perhaps more intelligent than Mary.

他或許比瑪麗更聰明。

3. Wedding Customs in Taiwan and in the USA

The wedding customs in Taiwan and in the United States are different. In Taiwan, the preparation of wedding includes an official proposal and the selection of an auspicious date. On the wedding day, the groom comes to the bride's house. The bride thanks her parents for the care and upbringing, and then her father covers the bridal veil. The couple leaves for the groom's home. At the groom's house, they worship the ancestors and the bride becomes a new member of the family. After the ceremony, the wedding reception is held at a restaurant or community hall. A typical reception banquet consists of ten courses of delicious food. Guests are expected to❶ give gifts of

money in red envelopes. On the other hand, in the United States, a bachelor party or a bachelorette party will be held before the wedding. The wedding ceremony takes place at a church. The bride's father accompanies her to walk down the aisle and hand[2] her to the groom. The couple declares wedding vows and exchanges wedding rings, a symbol of love and commitment to each other[3]. Finally, the bride throws her bouquet to the unmarried girls. The ceremony is followed by a reception, where a wedding cake, food, and drinks are provided. Friends give gifts, instead of money, to the couple to establish a new home. Therefore, the wedding ceremony, reception, and gift-giving customs are very different in Taiwan and in the United States.

台灣和美國的婚禮習俗

　　台灣和美國的婚禮習俗是不同的。在台灣，婚禮的準備包括正式的提親和選擇吉日。婚禮當天，新郎來到新娘家。新娘感謝父母的照顧和養育，然後父親為新娘蓋上頭紗。新郎新娘前往新郎的家。在那裡，他們祭拜祖先，新娘成為家裡的一個新成員。婚禮儀式結束後，在餐廳或社區禮堂宴客。一個典型的餐宴有十道美味的佳餚。客人給紅包禮金。另一方面，在美國，婚禮前會舉行告別單身派對。婚禮儀式在教堂舉行。新娘的父親陪她走教堂中間的走道，把她交給新郎。新郎新娘發表結婚誓言，交換結婚戒指，這象徵著彼此的愛與承諾。最後新娘拋出捧花給未婚女孩們。婚禮儀式後的餐宴有婚禮蛋糕、食物和飲料。好友送禮物，而不是金錢，給新郎新娘建立一個新的家庭。因此，台灣和美國的婚禮、宴客和送禮的習俗是很不同的。

段落結構▶

1.主題句（topic sentence）：第一句'The wedding customs in Taiwan and in the United States are different.'是主題句，指出台灣和美國的婚禮習俗是不同的。

2.支持句（supporting sentences）：介於主題句和結論句中間的句子都是支持句，本文採用block method，先寫台灣婚禮習俗（婚禮儀式、婚宴、送禮三方面）的特點，再寫美國婚禮習俗（婚禮儀式、婚宴、送禮三方面）的特點。

3.結論句（concluding sentence）：最後一句'Therefore, the wedding ceremony, reception, and gift-giving customs are very different in Taiwan and in the United States.'是結論句，重述主題句，台灣和美國的婚禮、宴客和送禮的習俗是很不同的。

字彙與片語 ▶

英　文	詞　性	中　文
wedding customs	*n. phr.*	婚禮習俗
official proposal	*n. phr.*	正式的提親
selection	*n.*	選擇
auspicious	*adj.*	吉祥的
groom	*n.*	新郎 = bridegroom
bride	*n.*	新娘
upbringing	*n.*	養育
cover	*v.*	蓋上
bridal veil	*n. phr.*	頭紗
leave for	*v. phr.*	前往
worship	*v.*	祭拜
ancestor	*n.*	祖先
ceremony	*n.*	儀式
reception	*n.*	宴客
typical	*adj.*	典型的
banquet	*n.*	餐宴
consist of	*v. phr.*	包括、組成
course	*n.*	一道菜
expect	*v.*	期待
red envelope	*n. phr.*	紅包
bachelor	*n.*	單身男子
bachelorette	*n.*	未婚女子
hold	*v.*	舉行（動詞三態hold, held, held）

英　文	詞　性	中　文
take place	*v. phr.*	舉行
accompany	*v.*	陪伴
aisle	*n.*	走道
declare wedding vows	*v. phr.*	發表結婚誓言
exchange wedding rings	*v. phr.*	交換結婚戒指
symbol	*n.*	象徵
commitment	*n.*	承諾
bouquet	*n.*	捧花
instead of	*prep. phr.*	而不是

文法解釋▶

❶ 語態分成主動與被動語態。通常會使用被動語態的情形，主要是語句中強調受事者為交談中心，或者施事者不是那麼重要、不需被說出來。不過，也有些情況下，動詞具有被動的意義，可是仍以主動的形式出現。我們以本文的範例做說明：

- The wedding ceremony takes place at a church.

➡ 本句語意上是被動語態，也就是說「婚禮被舉行」，不過，動詞片語 take place仍以主動形式出現。

- Guests are expected to give gifts of money in red envelopes.

➡ 'Guests'語意上是受事者，說話者想要強調的交談對象。語意上的施事者「主辦婚禮的人」是大家都知道的，但非交談中訊息傳達的重點。句法上主動與被動語態的變換如下：

161

　　　　　S　　V　　O

· They expect guests to give gifts of money in red envelopes.〔主動〕

· Guests are <u>expected</u> (by them) to give gifts of money in red envelopes.〔被動〕
　　　　　S　　V　　　　O

❷ ~ father accompanies her to walk down the aisle and *hand* her to the groom.　　　　　　　　　　　　　　　　　　　　v.　DO.　IO.

　　英文中有些常用的名詞有時可以當動詞用，像是hand（手（*n.*）／面交（*v.*））、chair（椅子（*n.*）／擔任主席（*v.*））、bag（袋子（*n.*）／裝入袋中（*v.*））。本句中hand作動詞用，直接受詞為her，間接受詞the groom前面有介系詞to。

❸ ~ exchanges wedding rings, *a symbol of love and commitment to each other*.

　　'a symbol of love and commitment to each other' 是wedding rings的同位語，有補充說明的意思。

4. Chinese Food and Japanese Food

　　Chinese food and Japanese food share some similarities but they are also different in many ways. One important similarity is that rice is the staple food in both China and Japan. A typical Chinese meal consists of rice, soup and side dishes of vegetables, meat or fish. Likewise, a traditional Japanese meal is rice, served with miso soup and side dishes. In addition, noodles are another basic food in both countries. Popular Japanese noodles include udon, served hot in soup,

and soba, served cold with dipping sauce. In China, noodles can be cooked in soup or stir-fried❶. Despite❷ the similarities, Chinese food and Japanese food are different in three aspects. One difference is that the Japanese love to eat sashimi, but in China, raw fish is not eaten as extensively as❸ in Japan. Another difference is the flavor. Chinese cuisine seems to have a stronger flavor, while Japanese cuisine tends to keep the natural flavors of the ingredients. The third difference is the dining style. A family-style dining, in which foods in large dishes are shared by everyone, is more common in China; however, an individual-style dining is preferred in Japan. The unique characteristics of both cuisines make them popular in the world.

中國菜和日本菜

　　中國菜和日本菜有著一些相似之處，但也有許多不一樣的地方。一個重要的相似點是，米飯是中國和日本的主食。一個典型的中國餐包含米飯、湯和配菜如蔬菜、肉或魚。同樣地，傳統的日本餐是米飯、味噌湯和配菜。還有，麵食也是這兩個國家另一個主食。受歡迎的日本麵包括烏龍麵：以熱湯食用，和蕎麥麵：以調味醬汁做成涼麵吃。在中國，麵條可煮成湯麵或炒麵。儘管這些相似之處，中國菜和日本菜在三個方面有所不同。一個不同點是日本人喜歡吃生魚片，但在中國，吃生魚片沒有像在日本那麼廣泛普遍。另一個不同點是味道。中國菜似乎比較重口味，而日本菜較傾向於保持天然原料的味道。第三個不同點是飲食方式。家庭式的飲食方式，就是菜餚放在大盤子上是由大家共享，在中國比較常見，但是日本人較喜歡個人式的飲食方式。這兩種菜餚獨有的特點使他們在世界上受歡迎。

段落結構 ▶

1.主題句（topic sentence）：第一句'Chinese food and Japanese food share some similarities but they are also different in many ways.'是主題句，指出中國菜和日本菜有著一些相似之處，但也有許多不一樣的地方。

2.支持句（supporting sentences）：介於主題句和結論句中間的句子都是支持句，先寫中國菜和日本菜的相同點，再比較兩者的不同點。

3.結論句（concluding sentence）：最後一句'The unique characteristics of both cuisines make them popular in the world.'是結論句，説明這兩種菜餚獨有的特點使他們在世界上受歡迎。

字彙與片語 ▶

英　文	詞　性	中　文
similarity	*n.*	相似之處
staple	*n.*	主食
	adj.	主要的
typical	*adj.*	典型的
consist of	*v. phr.*	包含
side dishes	*n. phr.*	配菜
likewise	*adv.*	同樣地
traditional	*adj.*	傳統的
serve	*v.*	提供服務
miso soup	*n.*	味噌湯
noodle	*n.*	麵食
basic	*adj.*	基本的
udon	*n.*	烏龍麵
soba	*n.*	蕎麥麵
dipping sauce	*n. phr.*	沾醬
stir-fried	*adj.*	炒的
despite	*prep.*	儘管
sashimi = raw fish	*n.*	生魚片
extensively	*adv.*	廣泛普遍
cuisine	*n.*	菜餚
flavor	*n.*	味道
tend to	*v. phr.*	傾向於

英　　文	詞　　性	中　　文
natural	*adj.*	天然的
ingredient	*n.*	原料、材料
dining style	*n. phr.*	飲食方式
common	*adj.*	常見的
prefer	*v.*	較喜歡
unique	*adj.*	獨有的
characteristic	*n.*	特點

文法解釋▶

❶ In China, noodles can be cooked in soup or stir-fried.

　　藉由本據我們補充幾個烹飪用語：stir-fry快炒，deep-fry油炸（食物完全浸在油裡），pan-fry用平底鍋煎。

❷ *Despite* the similarities, Chinese food and Japanese food are different in three aspects.

　　'despite'是一介系詞，「儘管」的意思，後面接名詞或名詞詞組，意義上相當於in spite of（儘管如此）。請看下面範例：

- *In spite of* the similarities, Chinese food and Japanese food are different in three aspects.

　　要注意的是：despite和although皆是儘管的意思，但despite後面只接名詞，不能接句子。Although連接兩個子句，用逗號連接。請看下面例句：

- *Despite* the similarities, Chinese food and Japanese food are different in three aspects.

= *Despite the fact that* Chinese food and Japanese food share some similarities,
   they are different in three aspects.

= *Although* Chinese food and Japanese food share some similarities, they are
   different in three aspects.

❸ ~ but in China, raw fish is not eaten *as extensively as* in Japan.

　　本句中'as extensively as'是副詞程度的比較，其比較級的句子結構如
下：

　　〔A＋動詞＋as＋原級形容詞或副詞＋as＋動詞＋B〕

　　要注意的是：比較的對象A和B在語意上必須是一致的。因此，範文的
句子事實上是省略了'it is eaten'，而代名詞it是替代'raw fish'。

　　- In China, raw fish is not eaten as extensively as (it is eaten) in Japan.

❹ **介系詞in的用法：**

　　a.表示位置、地方，有「在～之中」的意思：

　　　- ~ rice is the staple food *in* both China and Japan.

　　　- The unique characteristics of both cuisines make them popular *in* the world.

　　b.表示「關於、在～方面」的意思：

　　　- Chinese food and Japanese food share some similarities but they are also
     different *in* many ways.

　　c.表示形式、樣子，有「按～的形式」的含意：

　　　- In China, noodles can be cooked *in* soup or stir-fried.

　　　- Popular Japanese noodles include udon, servedhot *in* soup, ~.

5. Tablets and Laptops

Both tablets and laptops are portable computers, but they have many differences. An obvious **difference** is that a tablet has a touchscreen **while**[1] a laptop has a keyboard. One has to use the on-screen keyboard to input text on a tablet; **however**, many people cannot type as quickly on the touchscreen as they do on a physical keyboard. The second difference is the function. The functions of a tablet are limited. Tablets are used for entertaining purposes such as news or e-book reading, internet browsing, and film watching[2]. **On the contrary**, a variety of functions like word processing, multimedia presentation, and research can be performed on a laptop. The third difference is the size. Compared with a laptop, a tablet is smaller and lighter. It is easy to carry a tablet on trips. The last difference is that the storage capacity[3] of a laptop is larger than that of a tablet. A tablet is not capable of running programs that require large amounts of memory such as video editing. By[4] considering the different features of tablets and laptops, users decide which to buy based on their specific needs.

平板電腦和筆記型電腦

　　平板電腦和筆記型電腦皆是攜帶型的電腦，但他們有很多差異。一個明顯的差異是平板電腦有觸控螢幕而筆記型電腦有鍵盤。平板電腦需要使用螢幕上的鍵盤來輸入文字，但是很多人在觸控螢幕上打字沒辦法像在實體鍵盤上打字一樣快。第二個差異性是功能。平板電腦的功能是有限的，多用於娛樂用途如閱讀新聞或電子書、上網、看電影。相反地，筆記型電腦可進行多種功能如文書處理、多媒體演示、研究。第三個不同點是大小。與筆記型電腦相比，平板電腦更小更輕，旅行時很方便隨身攜帶。最後一個不同點是筆記型電腦的儲存容量大於平板電腦。平板電腦不能夠跑需要大量記憶體的程式，如影片編輯。使用者考慮平板電腦和筆記型電腦不同的特色，根據他們特定的需求決定買哪種電腦。

段落結構 ▶

　　1.主題句（topic sentence）：第一句'Both tablets and laptops are portable computers, but they have many differences.'是主題句，指出平板電腦和筆記型電腦皆是攜帶型的電腦，但有很多差異。

　　2.支持句（supporting sentences）：介於主題句和結論句中間的句子都是支持句，本文採用point-by-point method分別就keyboard, function, size, storage capacity各方面比較平板電腦和筆記型電腦的差異。

　　3.結論句（concluding sentence）：最後一句'By considering the different features of tablets and laptops, users decide which to buy based on their specific needs.'是結論句，建議使用者根據他們的需求來買電腦。

　　4.粗體字為表示兩者不同的用語：difference, while, however, on the contrary。

字彙與片語 ▶

英 文	詞 性	中 文
laptop	*n.*	筆記型電腦（攜帶型可放在腿上使用的電腦）
desktop	*n.*	桌上型電腦（放在桌上使用的電腦）
tablet	*n.*	平板電腦
portable	*adj.*	攜帶型的
touchscreen	*n.*	觸控螢幕
keyboard	*n.*	鍵盤
input	*v.*	輸入
text	*n.*	文字
function	*n.*	功能
limited	*adj.*	有限的
entertain	*v.*	娛樂
e-book	*n.*	電子書
internet browsing	*n. phr.*	上網
film	*n.*	電影
on the contrary	*phr.*	相反地
a variety of	*phr.*	多種
word processing	*n.*	文書處理
multimedia presentation	*n.*	多媒體演示
research	*n.*	研究
perform	*v.*	執行
compared with	*v. phr.*	與～相比
carry	*v.*	攜帶

英　文	詞　性	中　文
storage capacity	*n. phr.*	儲存容量
capable	*adj.*	能夠的
require	*v.*	需要
memory	*n.*	記憶體
feature	*n.*	特色
based on	*phr.*	根據
specific needs	*n.*	特定的需求

文法解釋▶

❶ An obvious difference is that <u>a tablet has a touchscreen</u> <u>while</u> <u>a laptop</u>

　　　　　　　　　　　　　　名詞子句1　　　　　　　　Conj. 名詞子句2

<u>has a keyboard.</u>

　　本句中while是表示反義的對等連接詞。

❷ Tabets are used for entertaining purposes such as e-book reading, internet browsing, and film watching.

　　其中e-book reading, internet browsing, film watching為對等的名詞片語。

❸ The last difference is that the *storage capacity* of a laptop is larger than *that* of a tablet.

　　本句裡'storage capacity'是由「名詞＋名詞」所形成的複合名詞。'storage'是一名詞，沒有相同意義的形容詞（比如像：beauty(Noun) - beautiful(Adj)），只好直接用名詞當作形容詞，修飾後面的名詞。同樣的例子

171

還有：

- language (Noun) professor (Noun)　　語言教師
- morning (Noun) paper (Noun)　　　　早報
- post (Noun) office (Noun)　　　　　　郵局

此外，形容詞的比較結構如下：〔～V + *more* + Adj. + *than* + ～〕，必須注意不可以弄錯比較對象，否則會造成意義上的不同，甚至語法上的錯誤。請看下面範例：

- I like you better than he (likes you).

我喜歡你勝於他（喜歡你）＝我比他更喜歡你。

➡ 本句是兩個主詞：I和he的比較。

- I like you better than him. ＝ I like you better than (I like) him.

我喜歡你勝於我喜歡他＝我比較喜歡你，而不是他。

➡ 本句是兩個受詞：you和him的比較。

- *The *storage capacity* of a laptop is larger than a tablet.（錯誤）

此句的錯誤在於比較對象：不應該把storage capacity（儲存容量）拿來和tablet（平板電腦）做比較。正確的說法如文章裡的原句：

- The storage capacity of a laptop is larger than *that* of a tablet.

➡ 'that'是the storage capacity的代名詞。

❹ *By* considering the ～, users decide which to buy based on their specific needs.

介系詞「by + 動名詞」表示方式和方法，意思是「藉由」。本句是用介系詞片語來組合句子，原本兩個句子：

Users consider the different features of tablets and latops.

Users decide which to buy based on their specific needs.

合併而成。

❺ **以下我們複習形容詞的比較級：**

　　a.形容詞最高級表達方式的句子結構如下：

　　➡️〔The＋形容詞最高級＋單數名詞＋be＋that＋子句〕

　　- The *most* important characteristic is that it never loses its appeal over time.

　　最重要的特色是隨著時間流逝它從未失去它的吸引力。

　　➡️〔...＋the＋形容詞最高級＋單數名詞＋of/among＋人或物（複數形）〕

　　- He is the most diligent boy among them.

　　他是他們之中最勤奮的孩子。

　　➡️〔...＋the＋形容詞最高級＋單數名詞＋that＋子句〕

　　- She is the best cook that I have ever heard.

　　她是我聽過最好的廚師。

　　- He is the best pianist that I have ever seen.

　　他是我見過最好的鋼琴家。

　　➡️〔... one of＋the＋形容詞最高級＋複數名詞＋that ...〕

　　- Bach was one of the greatest musicians that ever lived.

　　巴哈是有史以來最偉大的音樂家之一。

　　b.形容詞表達比較級的句子結構如下：

　　➡️〔主詞1＋動詞＋形容詞比較＋than＋主詞2〕

　　注意：單音節的形容詞字尾加-er，兩個以上的音節所組成的單字，
　　　　　其比較級是在形容詞原級的前面加上more（較多）或less（較
　　　　　少）。

- A table is smaller and lighter than a laptop.

平板電腦比筆記型電腦小而輕。

- She is more beautiful than Mary.

她比瑪麗雅漂亮。

- He is less intelligent than his elder brother.

他沒有他哥哥聰明。

c. 比較兩者優劣的例句：

- His grades were better than his elder brother's (= his elder's brother's grades).

他的成績比他哥哥好。

- Her grades were worse than mine (= my grades).

她的成績比我差。

- Our products are superior to theirs (= their products).

我們的產品比他們的好。

- Their products are interior to ours (= our products).

他們的產品比我們的差。

d. 形容詞表達同等比較級的句子結構如下：

➡ 〔主詞1＋動詞＋as＋形容詞原級＋as＋主詞2〕

- She is as beautiful as her sister.

她跟她姐姐一樣漂亮。

因果關係的段落
CAUSE & EFFECT PARAGRAPHS

因果關係的段落說明原因和結果的關聯性，也就是原因導致結果的段落。此類型的文章結構有兩種：

1.著重於原因：事情發生形成的原因（causes, reasons）是什麼，例如：探討網路購物受歡迎的原因是什麼。

2.著重於結果：某件事情導致什麼結果（effects, results），例如：探討科技進步對生活帶來的影響。

在因果關係的段落裡，表示原因的連接詞有：because, since, because of, due to, as a result of, on account of。表示結果的連接詞有：thus, therefore, as a result, consequently。

以下是比較與對比的段落我們提供的五篇範文。前三篇文章著重於原因（causes），第四篇及第五篇文章著重於結果（effects）。

第一篇文章 Why people like online shopping 探討網路購物受歡迎的原因

第二篇文章 Why people use Facebook 探討Facebook受歡迎的原因

第三篇文章 What causes obesity? 探討肥胖的原因

第四篇文章 Effects of Peer Pressure 探討同儕壓力的影響

第五篇文章 Effects of weather on our life 探討天氣對生活的影響

1. Why People Like Online Shopping

Online shopping is popular for several reasons. Convenience is the main reason that people shop online. Shoppers visit online stores and make purchases at their convenient time. They do not have to drive to the stores but sit in front of the computer, browse the internet, and choose what they want. If[1] people want to send gifts to friends, they only have to make orders online and the gifts will be delivered to their friends. Another reason is that consumers can compare prices among stores and read customer reviews on the websites. It[2] is easier for consumers to find out which shop offers the lowest price. Shoppers can also save money by finding discount coupons online. The third reason is that online shopping saves time and avoids crowds. Because many people shop during holidays, shoppers may need to wait for a long time until[3] the shop assistant can help or wait in line to pay for their purchases. The fourth reason is that a wider selection of products can be found in online stores than in local stores. Online stores provide more choices of brands and sizes than local stores. The last reason is that people have no pressure shopping online because no shop assistant is around to convince shoppers to make purchases. Because of[4] the above reasons, many people prefer online shopping to in-store shopping.

爲什麼人們喜歡網路購物

網路購物受歡迎有幾個原因。便利是人們上網購物最主要的原因。購物者在他們方便的時間到網路商店購買東西。他們不用開車,而是坐在電腦前、瀏覽網路、選擇他們想要的東西。如果想送禮物給朋友,只要在網路下訂單,禮品就會送到朋友手中。另一個原因是消費者可以比較各網路商店的價格和閱讀網站上的顧客評論。消費者能更容易找出哪家商店提供最低的價格。購物者也可以上網尋找折價券來省錢。第三個原因是網路購物節省時間和避免人潮。因爲很多人在假日出來購物,顧客可能需要等待很長一段時間直到店員可以來協助或是排隊等候付款。第四個原因是在網路商店可以找到比當地商店更廣泛的產品。網路商店比當地商店提供更多品牌和尺寸的選擇。最後一個原因是人們上網購物沒有壓力,因爲沒有店員在旁說服顧客進行購買。由於上述原因,許多人喜歡網路購物甚於店內購物。

段落結構 ▶

1.主題句(topic sentence):第一句'Online shopping is popular for several reasons.'是主題句,指出網路購物受歡迎有幾個原因。

2.支持句(supporting sentences):介於主題句和結論句中間的句子都是支持句,就每個原因convenience, money saving, time saving, selection of products, no pressure作說明。

3.結論句(concluding sentence):最後一句'Because of the above reasons, many people prefer online shopping to in-store shopping.'是結論句,重述主題句指出由於這些原因,許多人喜歡網路購物。

字彙與片語 ▶

英　文	詞　性	中　文
online shopping	*n. phr.*	網路購物
convenience	*n.*	便利
shopper	*n.*	購物者
online store	*n*	網路商店
make purchase	*v. phr.*	購買東西
browse the internet	*v. phr.*	瀏覽網路
make orders	*v. phr.*	下訂單
deliver	*v.*	送到
consumer	*n.*	消費者
compare	*v.*	比較
customer reviews	*n. phr.*	顧客評論
website	*n.*	網站
discount coupon	*n. phr.*	折價券
avoid	*v.*	避免
crowd	*n.*	人潮
shop assistant	*n.*	店員
wait in line	*v. phr.*	排隊
selection	*n.*	選擇
product	*n.*	產品
brand	*n.*	品牌
pressure	*n.*	壓力
convince	*v.*	說服
because of	*prep. phr.*	由於、因為
prefer... to...	*v. phr.*	喜歡…甚於…

文法解釋 ▶

❶ *If* people want to send gifts to friends, they only have to make orders online and ~.

　　本句*If*···所敘述的是事實，條件句的動詞語態用陳述式（直說法），表達肯定的語氣，而不是假設語態的動詞。

　　另外，假設語態的句型依時態可分成三種：「與未來事實相反」、「與現在事實相反」、「與過去事實相反」。假設語態的句子由兩個子句組成，一個是條件句另一個是主要子句。

　　a.與現在事實相反的假設法句子結構如下：

　　If＋S＋{were／過去式V}, S＋{should/would/could/might}＋原形V
　　　　　　　　條件子句　　　　　　　　　主要子句

　　- If I were a rich man, I would travel all over the world.
　　如果我是個有錢人，我會環遊世界。

　　➡事實是我不是有錢人，所以我也不會環遊世界。

　　b.與過去事實相反的假設法句子結構如下：

　　If＋S＋{had＋動詞過去分詞}, S＋{should/would/could/might}＋have＋動詞過去分詞
　　　　　　　　條件子句　　　　　　　　　主要子句

　　- If I had known that German was so difficult to learn, I would not have registered for this course.
　　如果我知道德文這麼難學，我不會選修它的。

c.與未來事實相反的假設法句子結構如下：

If + S + {were to + 原形V／過去式（與a相同）}, S + {should/would/ could/might} + 原形V

　　　　　　　　　　條件子句　　　　　　　　　　　　主要子句

- If I knew that you did not tell the truth, I would be very angry.

如果我知道你沒說實話，我會非常生氣。

➡本句需從上下文來判斷說話者要表達的是與未來事實相反或與現在
事實相反的假設法語句，因為兩者在句子結構上是一樣的。

- If the sun were to rise in the west, I would accept that job.

如果太陽從西邊出來，我就會接受那份工作。

➡事實是太陽不可能從西邊出來，我也不會接受那份工作。

❷ *It* is easier for consumers to find out which shop offers the lowest price.

　　It是虛主詞，用來強調後面這件事是容易的。It指的是to find out which shop offers the lowest price。本句亦可寫成如下：

- It is easier to find out which shop offers the lowest price.

❸ ~ shoppers may need to wait for a long time *until* the shop assistant can help or ~.

　　連接詞until或till意思是「一直到～」，不過，在肯定句和否定句表達的意思不一樣。請比較下面兩句：

- His mother asked him to clean the room and he did it *until* 23:00 last night.

他的母親要他整理房間，而他昨晚一直整理到23點。

- His mother asked him to clean the room and he did not do it *until* 23:00 last night.

他的母親要他整理房間，而他昨晚一直到23點才去整理。

以下是until用在否定句型的例句：

- I did not go to bed until 3:00am in the morning.

= It was not until 3:00am that I went to bed.

= Not until 3:00am did I go to bed.

昨晚我凌晨3點才上床睡覺。

- Children are not allowed to watch TV until they finish their homework.

= It is not until children finish their homework that they are allowed to watch TV.

= Not until children finish their homework are they allowed to watch TV.

孩子寫完功課才能看電視。

❹ *Because of* the above reasons, many people prefer online shopping to in-store shopping.

'because of'是介系詞片語，後面接名詞或名詞詞組，而'because'是一連接詞，後面接子句。請看下面例句：

- I did not go to play tennis because of rain.

因為下雨，我沒有去打網球。

- I did not go to play tennis because it rained.

因為下雨，我沒有去打網球。

2. Why People Use Facebook

Facebook is a popular social media network for three reasons. An important reason is that it provides a platform for users to keep in touch with their friends online. Users create a personal profile and interact with friends by chatting, sending messages, and sharing photos. Users also receive automatic notifications when their friends update their profiles. Another[1] reason is that it allows users to create common interest groups where[2] the members exchange information, post events, upload files, and discuss certain issues. People can also become fans of their favorite bands or organizations by joining the groups. Fans have access to the events and updates posted[3] on the pages. Finally, it is a useful online marketing tool. Owners of small business or large corporations can start Facebook pages and set up profiles to promote their products to the public. Facebook allows business owners to have conversations with customers and post photos and videos of the products. Advertising on the Facebook is a good way to reach a wide audience all over the world. Therefore, building[4] relationship, joining in clubs, and marketing are the three important features that make Facebook a popular social networking site.

為什麼大家使用Facebook

　　Facebook是個受歡迎的社交媒體網絡，原因有三點。一個重要原因是它提供了一個讓用戶與他們朋友在網路上保持聯絡的平台。用戶建立個人檔案，與朋友互動、聊天、發送消息、並分享照片。當朋友更新個人資料時，用戶也能自動收到通知。另一個原因是它允許用戶建立共同興趣的社群，成員能交換資訊、張貼事件、上傳文件和討論某些議題。用戶也能藉由參加社群成為他們喜愛的樂隊或團體的粉絲。粉絲可以獲取網頁上的活動訊息和資訊更新。最後，它是一個好用的網絡行銷工具。小型企業或大型企業的老闆可以設立Facebook網頁，建立檔案向大眾推銷自己的產品。企業業主透過Facebook與客戶交談、發布產品的照片和影帶。在Facebook廣告是一個把資訊傳遞到世界各地很好的方式。因此，建立關係、加入社群、行銷是三個使Facebook成為受歡迎的社交網絡的重要特色。

段落結構 ▶

　　1.主題句（topic sentence）：第一句'Facebook is a popular social media network for three reasons.'是主題句，指出Facebook受歡迎的原因有三點。

　　2.支持句（supporting sentences）：介於主題句和結論句中間的句子都是支持句，就每個原因building relationship, joining in clubs, marketing作說明。

　　3.結論句（concluding sentence）：最後一句'Therefore, building relationship, joining in clubs, and marketing are the three important features that make Facebook a popular social network.'是結論句，重述主題句強調這三個原因使Facebook成為受歡迎的社交網絡。

字彙與片語 ▶

英　文	詞　性	中　文
social media network	*n. phr.*	社交媒體網絡
platform	*n.*	平台
keep in touch	*v. phr.*	保持聯絡
profile	*n.*	檔案
receive	*v.*	收到
automatic	*adj.*	自動的
notification	*n.*	通知
update	*v.*	更新
	n.	更新
common	*adj.*	共同的
interest	*n.*	興趣
groups	*n.*	社群、團體
exchange	*v.*	交換
post	*v.*	張貼
upload	*v.*	上傳
fans	*n.*	粉絲（複數）
band	*n.*	樂隊
organization	*n.*	團體
have access to	*v. phr.*	獲取
marketing	*n.*	行銷
corporation	*n.*	公司、企業
promote	*v.*	推銷
product	*n.*	產品

英　文	詞　性	中　文
the public	*n.*	大眾
advertise	*v.*	廣告
all over the world	*adv. phr.*	世界各地
feature	*n.*	特色

文法解釋▶

❶ *Another* reason is that it allows users to create common interest groups ~.

another是不定代名詞，有下面幾個意思：

a. 再一個（＝one more）

- If you still feel sleepy, take another coffee.

　如果你仍然想睡覺，再喝一杯咖啡。

b. 另一個（＝a different one）

- There is a crack in this cup, show me another.

　這杯子有個裂痕，讓我看看另一個。

c. 同樣一個（＝also one）

- He is a fool, and you are another.

　他是個傻瓜，你也是個傻瓜。

❷ Another reason is that it allows users to create <u>common interest</u> <u>groups</u> *where* the members exchange information, post events, upload files, and discuss certain issues.

‘where’是關係副詞，兼有連接詞的功用，用於表示地方的名詞或表示

抽象概念的位置（亦即common interest groups）之後，引導形容詞子句（本句虛線的部份）。

　　關係副詞和關係代名詞的主要功能都是引導形容詞子句，不過關係副詞句法上是作副詞用，關係代名詞則是具有代名詞的功用。試比較下面的句子：

- This is the school *where* I was working.（正）
- This is the school which I was working.（誤）

〔本句關係代名詞which加上in，句法功用上等於關係副詞where: *This is the school in which I was working.*〕

- This is the museum where I visited last Sunday.（誤）

〔where不具有代名詞的功用，不能當形容詞子句裡動詞visited的受詞〕

- This is the museum *which* I visited last Sunday.（正）

❸ Fans have access to the events and updates *posted* on the pages.

　　本句可改寫成如下：關係代名詞which引導形容詞子句，也就是說，原句是省略了which are，留下posted，動詞的過去分詞當形容詞用，修飾前面的先行詞。

= Fans have access to the events and updates *(which are) posted* on the pages.

　　　　　　　　　　先行詞　　　　　　　　關係形容詞子句

❹ Therefore, *building* relationship, *joining* in clubs*, and marketing* are the three important features that make Facebook a popular social networking site.

　　動名詞具有名詞的性質，在句中可當主詞（例如本句虛線部份）。

3. What Causes Obesity?

Obesity is a global health problem, and the causes can be attributed to[1] unhealthy dieting styles, lack of exercise, and genetics. Unhealthy[2] eating styles like eating fast food and eating snacks at night contribute to obesity. Fast food is high in calories, fat, and sugar. People who eat snacks at night are likely to skip breakfast in the morning. For convenience, people also eat pre-packaged food or processed food that is harmful to health. Another cause is lack of exercise. Many office workers sit at desks for long hours without moving around. After work, they watch television, surf the internet, or play computer games. As a result, they take in more calories than they need, and the extra calories are stored as fat. Finally, studies show that genetics is linked to obesity. It takes longer for obese people to burn up calories because of certain genetic traits. People whose[3] family members are overweight may be at a higher risk of becoming overweight. Therefore, it is suggested[4] that people live a healthy lifestyle by eating vegetables and fish, cutting down on fat and sugar intake, and keeping regular exercises.

肥胖的原因

　　肥胖是一個全球性的健康問題，其原因可歸為不健康的飲食方式、缺乏運動以及遺傳。不健康的飲食方式如吃速食食物和晚上吃零食導致肥胖。速食食物的熱量、脂肪和糖分含量高。晚上吃零食的人有可能在早上不吃早餐。為了方便，人們也吃預包裝食品或加工食品，這對健康是有害的。另一

個原因是缺乏運動。許多上班族長時間坐在桌前沒有走動。下班後,他們看電視、上網或玩電腦遊戲。因此,他們吃進去的熱量比他們需要的多,多餘的熱量儲存爲脂肪。最後,研究指出基因與肥胖有關聯性。由於某些遺傳特性,肥胖的人需要較長的時間燃燒熱量。家庭成員有人過重的話,可能肥胖的風險較高。因此,建議人們要有健康的生活方式,吃蔬菜和魚,減少脂肪和糖分的攝取,並保持規律的運動。

段落結構 ▶

1.主題句(topic sentence):第一句'Obesity is a global health problem, and the causes can be attributed to unhealthy dieting styles, lack of exercise, and genetics.'是主題句,指出肥胖的原因有三個:不健康的飲食方式、缺乏運動、遺傳。

2.支持句（supporting sentences）：介於主題句和結論句中間的句子都是支持句，就每個原因unhealthy dieting styles, lack of exercise, genetics作說明。

3.結論句（concluding sentence）：最後一句'Therefore, it is suggested that people live a healthy lifestyle by eating vegetables and fish, cutting down on fat and sugar intake, and keeping regular exercises.'是結論句，建議人們要有健康的生活方式來解決肥胖的問題。

字彙與片語 ▶

英　文	詞　性	中　文
obesity	*n.*	肥胖
global	*adj.*	全球的
be attributed to	*v. phr.*	歸因於
dieting styles	*n. phr.*	飲食方式
genetics	*n.*	遺傳、遺傳學
snack	*n.*	零食、點心
contribute to	*v.*	導致
calories	*n.*	熱量、卡路里
fat	*n.*	脂肪
skip	*v.*	跳過（省去的意思）
pre-packaged	*adj.*	預包裝的
processed	*adj.*	加工的（動詞過去分詞作形容詞）
harmful	*adj.*	有害的
move around	*v. phr.*	走動
as a result	*conj.*	結果、因此

英　文	詞　性	中　文
store	*v.*	儲存
study	*n.*	研究（複數studies）
is linked to	*v. phr.*	有關聯 = is related to
obese	*adj.*	肥胖的
burn up	*v. phr.*	燃燒
because of	*phr.*	由於
genetic	*adj.*	基因的、遺傳的
trait	*n.*	特徵
overweight	*adj.*	過重的
at a higher risk of	*prep. phr.*	～較高風險
cut down on	*v. phr.*	減少
intake	*n.*	攝取
regular	*adj.*	規律的

文法解釋▶

❶ ~ the causes of obesity can *be attributed to* unhealthy dieting styles, lack of exercise, and genetics.

句型：S＋attribute結果to原因。請看下面例句：

He attributed his success to hard-work.

他把成功歸因於努力工作。

The doctor attributed her death to an unknown virus.

醫生把她的死亡歸因於不明病毒的感染。

❷ 有些形容詞若加上字首：un-, im-, in-, ir-, il-, dis-, 則變成帶有否定意味的相反詞。請看下列範例：

un-: unhappy（不快樂的），unhealthy（不健康的）

im-: impossible（不可能的），impatient（沒耐心的的）

in-: inexpensive（花費不多的），independent（獨立的、不依賴的）

ir-: irresponsible（不負責任的），irrelevant（不相關的）

il-: illegal（不合法的），illogical（不合乎邏輯的）

dis-: dishonest（不誠實的），disoriented（迷失方向的）

❸ People *whose* family members are overweight may be at a higher risk of becoming overweight.

　　句法上關係代名詞具有連接詞的功用，引導形容詞子句。本句whose是who的所有格關係代名詞，相當於of which引導的形容詞子句表達先行詞之所有格。請看下面範例說明：

I have a teacher. His father is a famous psychiatrist.

= I have a teacher whose father is a famous psychiatrist.

我有一位老師（他）的父親是有名的精神科醫生。

❹ ~ *it is suggested* that people *live* a healthy lifestyle by eating vegetables and fish, ~.

　　suggest是意志動詞，其句型為S1 + suggest + that + S2 + (should) + 原形動詞~。

　　如本文的句子It is suggested that people (should) live a healthy lifestyle by ~（省略should）

　　請再看以下例句：The doctor suggested that she (should) exercise every day.

　　其它意志動詞如：recommend, advise, ask, demand, insist, command等，句型皆為S1 + suggest + that + S2 + (should) + 原形動詞~。

191

此外，'It is + adj + that ～' 句型表説話者主觀的意見，認爲應該這樣做。子句裡的助詞可以省略不説。

- It is better that + S + (should) + V ～（最好……）
- It is good that + S + (should) + V ～（好的……）
- It is important that + S + (should) + V ～（重要的……）
- It is necessary that + S + (should) + V ～（必要的……）
- It is essential that + S + (should) + V ～（必要的……）

另外，'It is + pp + that ～' 句型亦可以用於表示客觀説法的句型，差別主要在於句中形容詞或過去分詞的含義不同，也就是説它們意義上是表達非主觀建議的，子句裡無須使用助動詞should。請看下面例子：

- It is agreed that + S + V ～（大家同意……）
- It is assumed that + S + V ～（假設……）
- It is believed that + S + V ～（大家相信……）
- It is hoped that + S + V ～（大家希望……）
- It is supposed that + S + V ～（有人推測……）
- It is said that + S + V ～（據説……）

➤It is said that his father was a famous doctor in his country.
據説他父親在他的國家是一位有名的醫生。

4. Effects of Peer Pressure

Peers have a great influence on each other. The effects of peer pressure can be positive or negative. One positive effect is that[1] peers are role models. When one sees that his friend joins a speech contest or takes part in a sport competition, he will be motivated to follow the example. Because students want to be like peers they admire, they will work hard to achieve the same goal. Another positive effect is that peers help each other develop similar interests. Students may become interested in music, art, or sports because of the influence of peers. Peers also encourage the participation of extracurricular activities, such as[2] joining clubs and doing volunteer work. However, peers also have negative effects. Students are influenced by peers to skip classes, cheat, or even use drugs or alcohol. Because they are worried that they are not accepted by the group, they behave the same way as[3] their peers do. Consequently, one does something that is contrary to his own belief or even does something illegal. In brief, although positive peer pressure is beneficial to students' learning, negative peer pressure may result in serious consequences.

同儕壓力的影響

同儕有很大的影響。同儕壓力有正面和負面的效果。正面的影響是同儕是學習的榜樣。當有人看到他的朋友參加演講比賽或運動比賽，會讓他有仿效的動力。因為學生想要跟他們欣賞的同儕一樣，他們會努力來達到同樣的目標。另一個正面效果是，同儕互相培養相同的興趣。因為同儕的影響，學

生可能對音樂、美術、體育產生興趣。同儕也會鼓勵彼此參與課外活動，如參加社團和做志工。不過，同儕壓力也有負面影響。同儕影響學生翹課、作弊、甚至吸毒或酗酒。因為他們擔心不被同儕接受，所以跟同儕有一樣的行為，因此可能做出一些違背自己信念或甚至違法的事。簡言之，雖然同儕壓力有利於學生的學習，也可能導致嚴重的後果。

段落結構▶

1.主題句（topic sentence）：第一句'Peers have a great influence on each other.'是主題句，指出同儕有很大的影響。

2.支持句（supporting sentences）：介於主題句和結論句中間的句子都是支持句，說明同儕壓力的正面影響和負面影響。

3.結論句（concluding sentence）：最後一句'In brief, although positive peer pressure is beneficial to students' learning, negative peer pressure may result in serious consequences.'是結論句，總結同儕壓力有利於學生的學習，也可能導致嚴重的後果。

字彙與片語▶

英 文	詞 性	中 文
influence	*n.*	影響
effect	*n.*	影響、效果
peer pressure	*n. phr.*	同儕壓力
positive	*adj.*	正面的
negative	*adj.*	負面的
role model	*n. phr.*	榜樣

英　文	詞　性	中　文
speech contest	*n. phr.*	演講比賽
competition	*n.*	比賽、競爭
motivate	*v.*	使～有動力
admire	*v.*	欣賞
achieve	*v.*	達到
encourage	*v.*	鼓勵
participation	*n.*	參與
extracurricular activities	*n. phr.*	課外活動
volunteer	*n.*	志工
skip classes	*v. phr.*	翹課
drug	*n.*	毒品
alcohol	*n.*	酒精
behave	*v.*	行為表現
consequently	*adv.*	因此
contrary	*adj.*	相反的
belief	*n.*	信念
illegal	*adj.*	違法的
beneficial	*adj.*	有利的
result in	*v. phr.*	導致
consequence	*n.*	後果

文法解釋 ▶

❶ One positive effect is *that* peers are role models.

'that'是從屬連接詞，引導名詞子句。

❷ Peers also encourage the participation of extracurricular activities *such as* joining clubs and doing volunteer work.

'such as'是解釋的副詞連接詞，後面接名詞詞組，不接句子。請再看下面範例：

- I need some books of references, such as a dictionary, a encyclopedia, etc.

我需要一些參考書，像是字典、百科全書等等。

❸ ~ they behave the same way *as* their peers do.

'as'是表方式的從屬連接詞。請再看下面範例：

- Do in Rome as the Romans do.

入境隨俗。

❹ 藉由本文，我們介紹英文介系詞的形式：

➡一般介系詞：in、on、with、to、for...。

➡介系詞片語

in brief	簡言之
in charge of	負責、管理
in front of	在～前面
in favor of	贊成、支持
in spite of	儘管
by means of	藉由

by way of	經由
in case of	萬一、假使
with respect to	關於

➡介系詞與動詞組合成的片語：「動詞＋介系詞」

account for	說明
divide into	分成
focus on	把重心放在～
begin with	以～開始
participate in	參加
consist of	由～組成
prepare for	準備～
deal with	處理、應付
rely on	依靠、倚賴
respond to	對～回應
result from	起因於～
depend on	視～而定
result in	導致、造成

➡介系詞與形容詞組合成的片語：「形容詞＋介系詞」

accustomed to	習慣於
beneficial to	有利於
contrary to	對立
interested in	對～有興趣
afraid of	害怕
identical to	與～完全相同

angry with	對人生氣
superior to	優於
inferior to	劣於
married to	娶～、嫁給～
next to	緊臨、僅次於
based on	以～爲根據
related to	與～有關
responsible for	爲～負責
similar to	與～相似
different from	與～不同

5. Effects of Weather on Our Life

Weather affects our life in many ways. First, it affects the kinds of sports or activities we can do. In summer, water sports like swimming, snorkeling, and surfing are popular activities for us to cool off. In winter, we may want to work out in the gym as it is cold outside. We can also go skiing in countries that❶ have snow. In addition, outdoor games are affected by the weather. Some sports events such as baseball games and tennis tournaments have to be cancelled on a rainy day. Second, the weather influences the food we can grow and eat. For example, tropical fruits like bananas, mangos, and papayas grow in warmer parts of the world. Vegetables such as cabbage and spinach grow in low temperature. Moreover, a higher level of humidity is required for leafy vegetables while a low level of humidity is better for fruits. Third, the weather influences our eating habits. When the weather is hot, we may lose appetite and eat less.

When it is cold, we tend to eat more because we need calories to stay warm. For instance, we like salads or ice cream in summer, and hot soup or hot chocolate in winter. To summarize, weather has an effect on the activities we do, the food we grow, and our eating habits.

天氣對生活的影響

　　天氣影響我們生活許多方面。第一，它影響我們可以做的運動或活動種類。在夏天，游泳、浮潛、衝浪等水上運動是我們消暑的熱門活動。在冬天，我們可能想在健身房做運動因為外面天氣冷。我們也可以去有雪的國家滑雪。此外，戶外活動比賽受天氣的影響。一些體育賽事如棒球比賽和網球錦標賽在下雨天會被取消。第二，我們所種植和食用的食物生長在不同的氣候下。例如，香蕉、芒果、木瓜等熱帶水果生長在溫暖的地區。蔬菜如高麗菜和菠菜生長在低溫環境。此外，葉菜類蔬菜需要濕度高的環境，而水果較適合濕度低的環境。第三，天氣影響我們的飲食習慣。當天氣炎熱時，我們可能較沒有食慾而吃的少。天氣冷的時候，我們往往吃較多因為我們需要熱量來保持體溫。例如，我們夏天喜歡吃沙拉或冰淇淋，冬天喜歡喝熱湯或熱巧克力。總之，天氣影響我們做的活動、種植的食物、和飲食習慣。

段落結構 ▶

　　1.主題句（topic sentence）：第一句'Weather affects our life in many ways.'是主題句，指出天氣影響我們生活許多方面。

　　2.支持句（supporting sentences）：介於主題句和結論句中間的句子都是支持句，分別說明天氣在activities, food, eating habits的影響。

　　3.結論句（concluding sentence）：最後一句'To summarize, weather has an

effect on the activities we do, the food we grow, and our eating habits.'是結論句，
重述主題句強調天氣在我們生活上的影響。

字彙與片語 ▶

英　文	詞　性	中　文
affect	*v.*	影響
water sports	*n. phr.*	水上運動
snorkeling	*n.*	浮潛
surfing	*n.*	衝浪
cool off	*v. phr.*	消暑
work out	*v. phr.*	做運動
gym	*n.*	健身房
outdoor	*adj.*	戶外的
tournament	*n.*	比賽、錦標賽
cancel	*v.*	取消
influence	*v.*	影響
tropical fruits	*n. phr.*	熱帶水果
cabbage	*n.*	高麗菜
spinach	*n.*	菠菜
temperature	*n.*	溫度
humidity	*n.*	濕度
require	*v.*	需要
leafy vegetables	*n. phr.*	葉菜類蔬菜
eating habits	*n. phr.*	飲食習慣

英　　文	詞　　性	中　　文
appetite	*n.*	食慾
calories	*n.*	熱量
summarize	*v.*	作總結
effect	*n.*	影響、效果

文法解釋▶

❶ 關係代名詞的使用本書在相關篇章已說明其用法，在這兒我們就作一簡
單複習整理。

　　句法上，關係代名詞可以有下列幾種功能：

先行詞	主格	所有格	受格
人	who	whose	whom
事物	which	whose / of which	which
人和事物	that	——	that

下面我們舉例並作說明：

- The boy who (that) is talking to the teacher is our new classmate.

那個跟老師說話的男孩是我們的新同學。

➡關係代名詞為人且為主格，who可用that代替。

- Those students who finished homework may go out to play tennis.

那些做完家庭作業的學生可以出去打網球。

➡關係代名詞為人且為主格。

- The girl whose father is a judge is Mary.

那位父親是法官的女孩是瑪麗。

➡關係代名詞表示人且為所有格。

- The man whom you were talking to is the chairman of the department.

那位你跟他說話的人是系主任。

➡關係代名詞為人且為受格時（whom）可省略。

- We recruit the man whom you recommended to us.

我們聘用你推薦給我們的那個人。

➡關係代名詞為人且為受格時（whom）可省略。

- 關係代名詞限定與補述用法

本例句，關係代名詞who前面沒逗號，是限定的關係形容詞子句，用來限定那一位在西班牙念書的姐姐，同時暗示說話者還有其她的姐妹。

- My sister who studies in Spain will come back to Taiwan this summer.

我有一位在西班牙念書的姐姐，今年夏天要回來臺灣。

如果關係代名詞who前面有逗號，是非限定的關係形容詞子句，用來補充說明那一位姐姐，且只有一位。

- My sister, who studies in Spain, will come back to Taiwan this summer.

我姐姐在西班牙念書，今年夏天要回來臺灣。

➡關係形容詞子句與先行詞之間若有逗號，不可用that替代who：

（×）- My sister, that studies in Spain, will come back to Taiwan thi
　　　summer.

- that的用法

句法上，that當關係代名詞用來替代表人、事、物等關係代名詞（who, whom, which）。要注意的是that不可作所有格。請看下面範例：

- I need a man that (who) can understand Spanish to be my interpreter.
我需要一位懂西班牙語的人當我的口譯。

- Is the man (that / whom) you were talking to the chairman of the department?
那位跟你說話的人是系主任嗎？

➡介系詞後面不可使用that:

（✕）- Is the man to that you were talking the chairman of the department?

（○）- Is the man to whom you were talking the chairman of the department?

- This is the bicycle (that / which) my parents bought me.
這就是我父母買給我的腳踏車。

下列情況只能使用that

·先行詞之前有最高級時

- He is *the best* student that I have ever seen.
他是我見過最好的學生、

·先行詞前面有序數時：ex.、the first、the last和all、the only（唯一）、
the same（相同）、the very（正是那個），用that。

- She is always *the first* one that comes to the party.
她總是第一位來到宴會的人。

- This is the same car that I bought last year.
這部車和我去年買的車相同。

‧若是疑問句的開頭是who、which、what時用that。

- Who is the child that is crying over there?

那邊哭泣的小孩是誰？

附錄　Appendices

附錄1. 大寫規則

(1) 專有名詞的第一字母要大寫。例如：Taiwan、Spain等。

(2) 專有名詞的縮寫。例如：U.S.A.。

(3) 文章的每個句子第一個字母必須大寫。

(4) 引用句的第一個字母要大寫。例如：

My mother said, "Don't miss the bus."

(5) 人名、宗教的各種神聖稱號、專有名詞。例如：John、God、the Bible、World War II。

(6) 頭銜稱呼。例如：Mr. Wang、Capt. Lee。

(7) 節日、星期各日、月份。例如：Christmas、Monday、April。

(8) 書報、雜誌名稱。例如：The Little Prince、China Post。

(9) 公司、商標、品牌名稱。例如：Coca-Cola、CitiBank、Toyota。

(10) 國家、語言、民族、城市名稱。例如：Swiss、French、New York。

(11) 山川、海洋、島嶼、湖泊、河流。例如：Sun Moon Lake、Gulf of Mexico、Atlantic Ocean、Mount Everest。

(12) 街道、公路、名勝古蹟名稱。例如：Yellowstone National Park。

(13) 學校、政府機關、民間團體。例如：the Y.M.C.A.、the Executive Yuan。

附錄2. 標點符號的使用

寫作時，絕不可以輕忽標點符號的使用，只有正確地使用，才能準確地表達意思，避免語意不清，產生誤解或難以閱讀。下面我們列舉幾種最常用的標點符號做說明。

❶ 逗號(,)

a. 用來連接兩個句子。

- We expected him to come to the party, but he never showed up.

我們期待他來參加派對，但是他都沒有出現。

b. 用在直接稱呼後。例如：

- Luis, please come to my office.

路易士，請到我辦公室。

c. 句法上表同位語。例如：

- Camilo José Cela, a Spanish novelist, was awarded the 1989 Nobel Prize in Literature.

加米諾·荷西·賽拉，西班牙小說家，一九八九年獲得諾貝爾文學獎。

- Rafael Nadal, an excellent tennis player, has come back to the tourment this year.

拉法納達爾是位優秀的網球選手，今年再度回到菁英賽的賽事。

d. 用在直接引句之前，和報告動詞分隔。例如：

- The teacher said, "You should study hard."

老師說：「你們應該努力用功讀書。」

e. 用來分隔地址內容的項目、數字。例如：

  - 3F, NO.5, 24 Lane, 3 Section, Ren-Ai Road, Taipei.
  台北市仁愛路3段24巷5號3樓

f. 用來省略重複的單字或片語。例如：

  - My father is a doctor, and my mother, a housewife.
  我的父親是醫生，我的母親則是家庭主婦。

g. 用在信件稱呼、結尾語之後。例如：

  - Dear John,
  親愛的約翰

  - Yours sincerely,
  你誠摯的朋友

h. 用來分隔句子中插入的單字、片語或子句。例如：

  - I accept, if anyone can prove the truth, that he is not guilty.
  如果有人能證明事實，我接受他是無罪的。

  - Later, however, he made up his mind to leave.
  之後無論如何他決定離去。

i. 非限定的關係子句前後各用一個逗號來分隔。例如：

  - My cousin, who did not marry until forty, had his first baby born last week.
  我的表哥，他直到四十歲才結婚，上星期他的第一個寶寶出生了。

j. 用來分隔對比的單字、片語或子句。例如：

  - Please put these boxes under the table, not on the table.
  請把這些箱子放在桌子下面，不是桌子上面。

k. 附加問句前用逗號來分隔。例如：

- You bought a new car, didn't you?

你買了一部新車，不是嗎？

❷ 句號(.)

a. 用在一個具有完整意思的句子之後。這個句子的結構可能是祈使句、簡單句、並列複合句、從屬關係的複合句與帶有關係形容詞子句的複合句。例如：

- It's ten o'clock. Let's take a break.

十點鐘了。我們休息一下。

- He is an English teacher.

他是一位英文老師。

- He looked at me and asked what I needed.

他看著我，然後問我需要什麼。

- She called me while I was taking a shower.

她打給我時，我在洗澡。

- I have a brother who works in Germany.

我有一個在德國工作的兄弟。

b. 用在縮寫之後。例如：

- Mr. and Mrs. White   懷特先生與太太
- e.g. = for example   例如
- i.e. = that is   也就是說
- U.S.A. = United Sates of America 美利堅合眾國

❸ 分號(;)

a. 用來連接兩個句子。請注意用分號隔開的兩個句子,中間不可再加上連接詞。

- We expected him to come to the party; however, he never showed up.

= We expected him to come to the party. However, he never showed up.

= We expected him to come to the party, but he never showed up.

我們期待他來參加派對,但是他都沒有出現。

b. 用來區隔句子裡介紹的各個項目。例如:

- There were only three men elected to be the board of directors of the University: George White, the dean of College of Business; Tom Smith, the director of the Accounting Office, and Pedro Goodman, the chairman of the Center for General Education.

三位被選為大學董事會的理事分別是:喬治懷特,商管學院院長;湯姆史密斯,會計室主任;和背得羅古德曼,通識教育中心主任。

c. 幾個句子並置時,如要省略幾個句子中的動詞,可用分號隔開。例如:

- Mary lives in Madrid; Mariana, in Barcelona, and I, in Salamanca.

瑪麗住在馬德里;瑪麗安娜,住在巴塞隆納;我住在薩拉曼加。

❹ 冒號 (:)

a. 書名和副書名用冒號分開。例如:

- Spanish cooking: How to make mediterranean declicacies

西班牙烹飪:如何做出地中海風味佳餚

209

b. 冒號用於一個正式的引用之前。與前述逗號不同的是，如果引用比較正式的發言講話就要用冒號，一般情況下就用逗號。例如：

- The principal said: "An idle youth a needy age."

校長說：「少壯不努力，老大徒傷悲。」

c. 用於介紹後面列舉的內容。例如：

- This is my first time to travel abroad. My mother helped me pack my suitcase: clothes, toilet papers, several one dollar bills, and a checklist.

這是我第一次出國。我的母親幫我打包行李：衣物、衛生紙、一些一塊美元紙鈔和一張清單。

❺ 所有格符號、縮寫 (')

a. 用來表示名詞的所有格。例如：

- This store sells children's books and toys.

這家店賣小孩子的書和玩具。

b. 若名詞本身是s結尾，所有格符號加在s的後面。例如：

- James' car

詹姆士的車子

- witches' brooms.

女巫的掃帚

c. 寫作時不宜使用縮寫。例如：

- I've been to..., I'd like to...是口語的用法，不宜出現在寫作中。

附錄3. 英語九大詞類

　　英文分成九個詞類：名詞、形容詞、冠詞、代名詞、動詞、副詞、介詞、連接詞和感嘆詞。以下我們依序就這幾個詞類做簡單的介紹。

❶**名詞**：英文的名詞有單複數之分，名詞在句法功用上可擔任主詞或受詞。

- *Time* is like a river.
時間就像流水。

- I bought a *car*.
我買了一部車。

❷**形容詞**：英文的形容詞放在名詞前面修飾該名詞。形容詞有原級，比較級和最高級的區別。

- This is a new house.
這是間新房子。

- Mary is taller than I.
瑪麗比我高。

❸**冠詞**：英文有定冠詞〈the〉與不定冠詞〈a / an〉。the用在限定、特定的名詞前，a/an用在非限定、非特定的名詞前。試比較下面例句：

　　a. The red car in the exhibition hall looks cool. I am thinking to buy it.
　　　展覽館那輛紅色的車子看起來很酷，我想要買。「車」放在句首表主題的功用，限定用法，說話者與聽話者皆知道哪輛車。

b. I am thinking to buy a car.

　　我一直想買輛車。「車」放在動詞後面，若不帶任何指示代詞，表非限定用法，說話者沒有確切指出是哪輛車。

❹代名詞：英文的代名詞可再分為人稱代名詞（I, you, he, she, etc.）、指示代名詞（this, that, those, etc.）、疑問代名詞（waht, why, how, etc.）、關係代名詞（who, which, etc.）、不定代名詞（all, both, some, none, anybody, etc.）等。

❺動詞：英文的動詞算是較複雜的一項詞類，但與西班牙語、法語、德語比起來又簡單多了。動詞詞尾變化可以表示時態，而詞尾變化本身又可再分成規則變化與不規則變化。

- He was a bus driver.

他以前是公車司機。

- They found the truth.

他們發現事實了。

❻副詞：用來修飾、動詞、形容詞、或另一個副詞，有時也用來修飾名詞。

- The number of elderly people has rapidly increased in the past decade.

老年人口在過去十年快速增加。

（副詞rapidly修飾動詞increased）

- Mary and Sue are twins, but their personalities are completely different.

Mary和Sue是雙胞胎，但她們的個性完全不同。

（副詞completely修飾形容詞different）

- He rented out the rooms upstairs to students.

他把樓上的房間租給學生。

（副詞upstairs修飾名詞rooms）

❼介系詞：也是沒有詞尾變化的詞類，其功用主要是用來指明後面的受詞和前面的名詞或動詞之關係。通常出現在受詞的前面，所以又稱之爲「前置詞」。英文的介系詞有of, from, in, by, for, with, on, at, during, after, before, within, through, off, over, up, besides等等。

❽連接詞（Conjunctions）：用來連接簡單句裡的相等成分或複合句裡的各個組成句子，表明它們之間在語法上和邏輯上的關係。英文的連接詞分爲對等連接詞和從屬連接詞。我們分別列舉如下：

＜對等連接詞＞

- 累積式　and, both ... and ..., not only ... but also ..., as well as, neither ... nor ..., besides, moreover, furthermore, in addition, what is more, what is worse, etc.
- 選擇性　or, either ... or ..., otherwise, etc.
- 反　義　but, whereas, while, yet, etc.

＜引導名詞子句的從屬連接詞＞

that, whether, if, lest, whatever, whoever, whomever, whosever, etc.

＜引導形容詞子句的從屬連接詞＞

who; whom; whose; which; that; etc.

＜引導副詞子句的從屬連接詞＞

- 時　間　when, while, as, till, untill, since, after, before, as long as, once, by the time, not ... long before, no sooner ... than, as soon as, whenever, etc.

- 讓　步　if, whether or not, although, though, even though, even if, no matter what, while, whereas, etc.

- 目　的　so that, in order that, etc.

- 條　件　if, unless, as long as, in case, if only（只要）, only if（只有）, on condition that, provided that, etc.

- 原　因　because, as, considering that, since, for the reason that, etc.

- 結　果　so ... that ..., such ... that ..., etc.

- 地　點　where, wherever, etc.

- 比　較　than, the ... the ..., as ... as, not so ... as ..., etc.

❾驚嘆詞：Oh! Ouch! My goodness!

附錄4. 英語五大句型

　　寫作的方式與技巧千變萬化，寫作文體依作者本意可以是敘述、描寫、論說等等，儘管同一個主題每一個人寫出來的文章都不盡然相同，這也是我們常說的每個人都有屬於自己的文筆、寫作風格和創造性。但是寫作的最終目的是傳達作者本身的思想與意念，因此，清楚、明白才是一篇好文章的最根本條件，可是對很多人來講卻很困難，一方面是想太多，另一方面是錯誤的觀念，認爲用字越艱深，句子越長越複雜表示程度越好越有學問。如果我們聽聽畢卡索曾說過的一句：「小孩子的畫是最難學的」，就不難了解「簡單明瞭」反而是最高的境界。

　　英語寫作最終也是遵行著自身語言的句法規範，也就是下面我們列出的五大句型。熟悉這五大句型，不僅可以幫助我們寫出正確句子，在文章完成時亦提供我們一個句法檢查的準則。

❶ S＋V（主詞＋完全不及物動詞）

- The bus stopped.　　公車停下來了。
　　 S　　 V

此句型既不需要受詞也不需要補語。

　　動詞stop之後不須要接何字詞即可表達完整句意，這類動詞稱爲「完全不及物動詞」。

❷ S＋V＋SC（主詞＋不完全不及物動詞＋主詞補語）

- The picture is good.　　這幅畫很不錯。
　　 S　　 V SC

此句型不需要受詞，但是要有補語。

　　動詞is之後必須要接適當的字詞，像是名詞或形容詞才能表達完

整的句意，這類動詞稱爲「不完全不及物動詞」。本句中good是用來補充説明主詞的字稱爲「主詞補語」。

❸ S＋V＋O（主詞＋完全及物動詞＋受詞）

- John loves music.　　約翰喜愛音樂。
　　S　　V　　O

此句型不需要補語，但是要有受詞。

動詞love（喜愛）之後必須接名詞或名詞詞組：music（音樂），做句法上的受詞，才能表達完整的句意，這類動詞稱爲「完全及物動詞」。

❹ S＋V＋O＋OC（主詞＋不完全及物動詞＋受詞＋受詞補語）

- The King appointed him the prime minister.　　國王任命他爲總理。
　　S　　　V　　　O　　　OC

此句型需要受詞，也要有補語。

動詞appoint（指派）之後除了接名詞或代名詞之外，必須再接另一個字詞：prime minister（總理），補充説明句法上當受詞的人稱代名詞him，這樣的句意才完整，這類動詞稱爲「不完全及物動詞」。

❺ S + V + IO + DO（主詞 + 授與動詞 + 間接受詞 + 直接受詞）

- I <u>bought</u> <u>my sons</u> <u>some toys</u>. = I bought some toys for my sons.
  S   V   IO   DO

我給我兒子買些玩具。

　及物動詞buy（買）又稱為授與動詞，之後必須接兩個受詞，一是表示人的間接受詞my sons，另一個是表示物的直接受詞some toys。

附錄5. 英語的句子結構

按句子的結構，可以有簡單句、並列句和複合句。

A. 簡單句（simple sentences）

簡單句由一個主詞和一個動詞組成，動詞後面可帶也可不帶受詞或補語。動詞可以分成及物或不及物和無人稱。若動詞為及物，句型又可分為主動和被動語態。

例如：

- Mary is a nurse.

瑪麗是護士。

- Mary went home early today.

瑪麗今天很早回家。

- It rained cats and dogs.（無人的句子由it作虛主詞）

下起傾盆大雨。

- The king appointed him the prime minister.（主動）
- He was appointed as the prime minister by the king.（被動）

B. 合句（Compound Sentences）

合句是由兩個或多個子句組成的，這些獨立子句由對等連接詞連接。例如：

a. 累積式：

- Mary works during the day and has classes in the evening.

瑪麗白天工作，晚上仍然要上課。

b. 選擇式：

-You can choose to stay or quit.

你可以選擇留下或退出。

c. 反義式：

-John is not intelligent, but he works hard.

約翰模聰明，但他很努力工作。

d. 推理式：

- It is going to rain, so we have to hurry up.

快要下雨了，所以快點。

C. 複句（Complex Sentences）

複句一般是由主要子句和從屬子句組成。無論句法上或語意上，藉由從屬連接詞表現出句子彼此間存在著主從依附的關係。

a. 名詞子句：

- He promised that he would tell me the truth.

他答應會告訴我事實。

b. 關係形容詞子句：

- He has a sister who studies in New York.

他有一個在紐約工作的姐姐。

c. 不同的從屬連接詞引導的副詞子句：

- ● 時間　We went to the movies *after* we finished our homework.

我們做完家庭作業後去看電影。

- 地方　We visited the house *where* Mozart was born.

　　　　我們參選了莫札特出生的房子。

- 原因　I didn't go to play tennis *because* it rained.

　　　　我沒去打網球，因為下雨了。

- 方式　Do in Rome *as* the Romans do.

　　　　入境隨俗。

- 目的　She got up early *in order that* she could catch the train.

　　　　她很早起來以便能搭上火車。

- 條件　*If* you are ill, you should go to see a doctor.

　　　　如果你生病了，去看醫生。

- 讓步　*Although* he was poor, he was quite generous to his needy friends.

　　　　雖然他很窮，他對他需要（幫忙）的朋友仍相當慷慨。

- 結果　The bus was *so* full *that* I could hardly got off.

　　　　公車好擠以致於我幾乎無法下車。

- 比較　The storage capacity of a laptop is *larger than* that of a tablet.

　　　　筆記型電腦的儲存容量大於平板電腦。

附錄6. 英語句子的用途分類

A. 陳述句：單純地陳述事實，不帶有說話者主觀意念。

- He didn't go to school yesterday.

他昨天沒有去學校。

B. 感嘆句：表達讚美、高興、驚訝、痛苦等句型。

- How beautiful the girl is!

這女孩好漂亮！

C. 祈願句：表達希望、高興、驚訝、痛苦等句型。

- God bless you!

上帝保佑你！

D. 懷疑、疑問句：表懷疑、猜測。

- Can you drive a car?

你會開車嗎？

- Where are you from?

你是哪裡人？

- Is your car expensive or cheap?

你的車很貴還是便宜？

- She is a teacher, isn't she?

她是老師，不是嗎？

E. 祈使句、命令句

- Please be seated.

請坐。

附錄7. 縮寫

- *abbr.*   abbreviation（縮寫）
- *n.*   noun（名詞）
- *n. phr.*   noun phrase（名詞片語）
- *v.*   verb（動詞）
- *v. phr.*   verbal phrase（動詞片語）
- *adj.*   adjective（形容詞）
- *adj. phr.*   adjective phrase（形容詞片語）
- *adv.*   adverb（副詞）
- *adv. phr.*   adverbial phrase（副詞片語）
- *prep.*   preposition（介系詞）
- *prep. phr.*   prepositional phrase（介系詞片語）
- *conj.*   conjunction（連接詞）
- *DO*   direct object（直接受詞）
- *IO*   indiect object（間接受詞）
- *SC*   subject complement（主詞補語）
- *OC*   object complement（受詞補語）

附錄8. 漢語拼音對照表

➡ 35個韻母與其國字範例（含母音、雙母音）

注音符號 (AFN)	漢語拼音 (Pinying)	國際音標 (AFI)	國字範例
ㄧ	y, i	i	醫
	i	i	帀
ㄨ	w, u	w	嗚
ㄩ	u	y	淤
ㄚ	a	ɑ	阿
ㄛ	o	o	喔
ㄜ	e	ɤ, ə	痾
ㄝ	e	e	耶
ㄦ	er	ɚ	兒
ㄞ	ai	aɪ	曬
ㄟ	ei	eɪ	杯
ㄠ	ao	ɑʊ	枒
ㄡ	ou	oʊ	歐
ㄢ	an	an	安
ㄣ	en	ən	恩
ㄤ	ang	ɑŋ	骯
ㄥ	eng	əŋ	亨
ㄧㄠ	iao		邀
ㄧㄡ	iu		優
ㄧㄢ	ian		煙

注音符號 (AFN)	漢語拼音 (Pinying)	國際音標 (AFI)	國字範例
一ㄚ	ia		壓
一ㄝ	ie		噎
一ㄣ	in		因
一ㄤ	iang		洋
一ㄥ	ing		應
ㄨㄣ	un		瘟
ㄨㄤ	uang		汪
ㄨㄥ	ong		翁
ㄨㄞ	uai		歪
ㄨㄟ	ui		威
ㄨㄢ	uan		灣
ㄨㄚ	ua		挖
ㄨㄛ	uo		倭
ㄩㄢ	uan		冤
ㄩㄝ	ue		約
ㄩㄥ	iong		雍
ㄩㄣ	un		暈

➤ 22個子音與其國字範例

注音符號 (AFN)	漢語拼音 (Pinying)	國際音標 (AFI)	國字範例
ㄅ	b	p	把
ㄆ	p	p^h	爬
ㄇ	m	m	媽
ㄈ	f	f	飛
ㄉ	d	t	帝
ㄊ	t	t^h	頭
ㄋ	n	n	拿
ㄌ	l	l	累
ㄍ	g	k	哥
ㄎ	k	k^h	渴
ㄏ	h	x	好
ㄐ	j	tɕ	教
ㄑ	q	$tɕ^h$	妻
ㄒ	x	ɕ	希
ㄓ	zh	tʂ	支
ㄔ	ch	$tʂ^h$	吃
ㄕ	sh	ʂ	師
ㄖ	r	ʐ	日
ㄗ	z	ts	咨
ㄘ	c	ts^h	疵
ㄙ	s	s	思

225

國家圖書館出版品預行編目資料

英文段落寫作範例／陳怡真、王鶴巘著.
　－－初版.－－臺北市：五南，2014.05
　面；　公分.－－
　ISBN 978-957-11-7574-4（平裝）
　1.英語　2.作文　3.寫作法
　805.17　　　　　　　　103004582

1AH1

英文段落寫作範例

作　　　者 ― 陳怡真、王鶴巘

發 行 人 ― 楊榮川

總 編 輯 ― 王翠華

主　　　編 ― 朱曉蘋

封面設計 ― 童安安

出 版 者 ― 五南圖書出版股份有限公司

地　　　址：106台北市大安區和平東路二段339號4樓

電　　　話：(02)2705-5066　　傳　　　真：(02)2706-6100

網　　　址：http://www.wunan.com.tw

電子郵件：wunan@wunan.com.tw

劃撥帳號：01068953

戶　　　名：五南圖書出版股份有限公司

台中市駐區辦公室/台中市中區中山路6號

電　　　話：(04)2223-0891　　傳　　　真：(04)2223-3549

高雄市駐區辦公室/高雄市新興區中山一路290號

電　　　話：(07)2358-702　　傳　　　真：(07)2350-236

法律顧問　林勝安律師事務所　林勝安律師

出版日期　2014年5月初版一刷

定　　　價　新臺幣350元